Praise for *Cosmogony*

"I recommend Lucy Ives's inventive collection of complex, deadpan, analytical, interrelated, controlledly wandering stories about divorce, lies, fear, parents, memes, the Internet, art, artists, information, and literature."

—TAO LIN, author of *Trip* and *Taipei*

"Rare and fearless, *Cosmogony*'s high-wire formal playfulness forges a circuit of human connection blinking at unlikely nodes. Even in moments of alienation and hurt, Ives's characters find themselves inextricably tethered to each other through philosophy, systems that fail them, art and love and searching. The puzzle pieces of this collection notch together, assembling a picture of the mysterious intelligence of coincidence and the sad, funny faces with which we meet it."

—TRACY O'NEILL, author of *Quotients* and *The Hopeful*

Praise for *Loudermilk*

"This clever satire of writing programs exhibits, with persuasive bitterness, the damage wreaked by the idea that literature is competition."

—*The New York Times Book Review*, Editors' Choice

"Ives's interests point toward the philosophical, even the mystical. *Loudermilk* is not just funny; it becomes a layered

exploration of the creative process . . . Ives approaches the students themselves with canny tenderness, and their work (which the novel excerpts, delightfully) with grave respect. Her own language is prickly and odd, with a distracted quality, as if she were trying to narrate while another voice is murmuring in her ear."　　　　　　　　　—*The New Yorker*

"Ives, who once described herself as 'the author of some kind of thinking about writing,' examines the conditions that produce authors and their work while never losing a sense of wonder at the sheer mystery of the written word."

　　　　　　　　　　　　　　　　　—*Bookforum*

"In a literary critical flourish, [Ives] combines elements of libertine novels, realist novels, social novels, inherited wealth lit, postmodern novels, period pieces, poetry, satire, and revenge plots . . . A funny and cutting novel whose critiques of inherited wealth and its effects on culture in the aughts will keep being true until a full redistribution of wealth, beginning with reparations, occurs."　　　　　　—*The Nation*

"Readers expecting yet another referendum on the MFA will be pleasantly surprised to discover a much stranger and more ambitious book. In *Loudermilk*, Ives has taken a subject notoriously difficult to make interesting—the difficulty of writing itself—and narrativized it into an elaborate plot peopled by avatars of the types Sontag enumerated decades ago . . . Sontag says a good writer must be a fool and an obsessive, that the critic and the stylist are bonuses (so, inessential). But Ives—not just for her own erudition and syntactical artistry, remarkable as they are—counters that it is the critic and the stylist who are indispensable, for they are the ones who interface thought with language."

—*The Believer*

"Hilarious . . . A riotous success. Equal parts campus novel, buddy comedy and meditation on art-making under late capitalism, the novel is a hugely funny portrait of an egomaniac and his nebbish best friend." —*The Washington Post*

"Hilarious, pointed, perfectly executed . . . Ives manages to subvert all expectations, and offers up one of the slyest, smartest looks at what it means to be a writer I've read; her every sentence sings, and they're songs I'll return to again and again." —*NYLON*

"*Loudermilk*, a satire, explores a complex web of plot and episodes, thick descriptions, biting character arcs, poetic and philosophical precision, stylistically different stories/poems within stories, the nature of time, and the mirage of power (or the possibility of unveiling politics, and cracking open agency). By employing a classical theatrical technique of dramatis personae, rather than 'realistic' novel characters, perhaps Ives is able to move between so many registers that enable her unusual 'mash-up' to excel as at once philosophical and planted in the mud . . . Ives's style of satire shatters the dichotomy between meta-narrative and human empathy. Breaking such a distinction requires rare observational skill, patience, and multi-genre flexibility and curiosity."

—*The Brooklyn Rail*

"Ives's new novel is one of the funniest in recent memory, stuffed with jabs at writers and toxic masculinity, bluntly yonic allusions, and feuilleton-esque prose that prances on page . . . What Ives is playing with here is not just beautiful sentences and humorous situations, it's the disharmony felt at the core of our experiences . . . Though the empirical distinctions between prose and poetry are often illusory, Ives finds a way to make her prose both a kind of communication—as is expected—as well as a construction of satire. Her words linger longer than normal trade, and find ways to avoid their disintegration, as if the must of a punchline is more lasting, more fragrant; words this eloquently framed and humorous imprint, and, often enough, hold us in their absurdity."

—*The Adroit Journal*

"*Loudermilk* may best be read as a contribution to a growing body of literature that both historicizes and critiques the MFA program . . . Loudermilk suggests that MFA programs are only incidentally committed to the production of great writing, that their true purpose is the cultivation and maintenance of power. In this, they have been perversely successful—as successful as Loudermilk himself. And yet, paradoxically, their very success in cultivating such power has led the MFA into crisis." —*The Georgia Review*

"This send-up of contemporary graduate writing programs and the characters they attract and create is sure to highly amuse any reader, especially those with a penchant for academia-set hijinks. Reminiscent of Michael Chabon, this highly original satiric novel is sharp-witted and adroit. Brava." —*Addison County Independent*

"Lucy Ives mixes genres with unusual abandon in her second novel, *Loudermilk*. The narrative could be regarded as a campus novel, a portrait of the artist, a scam story, a retelling of *Cyrano de Bergerac*, or a farce . . . *Loudermilk* is a novel about the tension between art and life, and the conflict between labor and power." —*On the Seawall*

"The nuanced subversion of tropes and full-throttle self-indulgence of Ives's writing lend a manic glee to this slyly funny and deeply intelligent novel."
—*Publishers Weekly* (starred review)

"Ives's satirical masterpiece follows poet Troy Augustus Loudermilk, a shallow Adonis recently admitted to the nation's premiere creative-writing graduate program, located in the heart of America's starchy middle . . . Laugh-out-loud funny and rife with keen cultural observations, Ives' tale is a gloriously satisfying critique of education and creativity."

—*Booklist* (starred review)

"A book where profound poststructuralist meditations on language, chance and creativity are deftly spun through with a myriad of jokes about farting, sex and male anatomy . . . With the Bush presidency and invasion of Iraq playing out ambiently and calamitously in the background, *Loudermilk* perfectly captures the strange cultural ethos of the early 2000s . . . With razor-sharp prose and a plenitude of linguistic strangeness, Ives has written a novel about American college life that is both philosophically gripping and exceptionally hilarious."

—*Shelf Awareness* (starred review)

"Lucy Ives is as deeply funny and ferocious a writer as they come. She's also humane and philosophical when it matters most. I love *Loudermilk*." —SAM LIPSYTE

"With *Loudermilk*, Lucy Ives tears down the curtain to unveil the wizard—and here all of the characters are implicated in operating the clunky machinery that creates then lionizes the concept of merit or talent in the academic/literary world. The result is this wildly smart novel that hilariously exposes its characters as they try to vault or cement themselves into some literary canon and/or ivory tower, unaware that the canon/tower is an ever-vanishing mausoleum wherein living writers go to get stuck, or lost, or to scrawl their names and draw butts and boobs on the walls." —JEN GEORGE

Cosmogony

Cosmogony

Stories

Lucy Ives

Soft Skull
New York

This is a work of fiction. All of the characters, organizations, and events portrayed in this novel are either products of the author's imagination or are used fictitiously.

Library of Congress Cataloging-in-Publication Data
Names: Ives, Lucy, 1980– author.
Title: Cosmogony : stories / Lucy Ives.
Description: First Soft Skull edition. | New York : Soft Skull, 2021.
Identifiers: LCCN 2020031591 | ISBN 9781593765996 (paperback) | ISBN 9781593766047 (ebook)
Classification: LCC PS3609.V48 A6 2021 | DDC 813/.6—dc23
LC record available at https://lccn.loc.gov/2020031591

Cover design & Soft Skull art direction by
www.houseofthought.io
Book design by Wah-Ming Chang

Published by Soft Skull Press
1140 Broadway, Suite 704
New York, NY 10001
www.softskull.com

Printed in the United States of America
10 9 8 7 6 5 4 3 2 1

It is supernatural to stop time.

SIMONE WEIL, notes for *Venise Sauvée*

Contents

A Throw of the Dice   / 3

Cosmogony   / 35

Recognition of This World Is Not
    the Invention of It   / 53

Scary Sites   / 75

The Care Bears Find and Kill God   / 103

Bitter Tennis   / 121

Louise Nevelson   / 141

Trust   / 151

The Poisoners   / 161

Guy   / 179

The Volunteer   / 203

Ersatz Panda   / 219

Notes   / 233

Cosmogony

A Throw of the Dice

When we were first married, he went out and bought a ball gag. It wasn't something I asked him to do. He wasn't a tall man but I suppose he was reasonably strong. He had a construction job, at the time. It was the sort of work he claimed to prefer.

We were living in San Francisco and through some act of god managed to find an apartment we could afford in an occasionally fancy neighborhood. It was just two rooms with a kitchen, the bathroom memorable for its coordinating sink, tub, toilet, and floor-to-ceiling tile, all a click shy of Pepto-Bismol. Outside, in the mornings and at dusk, an oddly shaped vehicle I learned to call the Google Bus rolled darkly by.

He was up at five, cycling into the East Bay. Around

seven, when a neighbor made her daily foray, the garage door screwed into the ceiling that was also the floor beneath our bed (a mattress) went into action. It was a braying sound, accompanied by copious vibration. During this process, I envisioned what I believed to be the exact fashion in which the building would collapse during an earthquake. I saw myself mangled in rubble. I lay, intact within the intact building, in bed, possessed by vertigo.

I did not work in tech, either. I worked full time for an employment agency. I had originally gone in to temp but had been hired as the front-desk girl. An Australian man with outrageous good looks, benefiting from the immigration policies of President George W. Bush, had hired me, citing my unusual abilities as a typist. Although I insisted that I preferred something with fewer hours, the agency maintained that it was low on contracts and could I please take them up on this offer, seeing as I was unlikely to receive another.

Yes, I said.

Great, they replied. Wonderful.

"I am so pleased!" announced the Australian, glinting hugely. He really was astonishing, ranching in his family, eyes and teeth like polished rocks. He began telling a long, long story about his very young wife.

I thought all the time about how much I loved him. It would come to me as I was walking down the street. I loved him, the man I was married to, and, as well as being afraid of earthquakes, feared that one of us might die in a plane crash or be pulled down by a rogue wave. I thought of meningitis, serial killers, war. Fog rolled up the hill. It was night again.

I minced cilantro. We sat at our table by the window and had a beer.

He went on several shopping excursions. He returned with bags stuffed with violet tissue. He quietly reentered the house.

It was a Sunday.

He restrained me.

He was, as I was saying, not a large man. He was a relatively small man, and he was full of a searing rage, an odorless, colorless flame, unknowable to the naked eye. We'd take the BART to a party and pass card tables set up by proselytizing Scientologists, and he would explain that they believed all humans were animated by the souls of aliens long ago subject to genocide.

I wanted to take the stress test, but he wouldn't let me. "L. Ron Hubbard was like, I'm going to invent a truly stupid religion. Look at these people," he said. He seemed not to want to get too close to them, but I noticed a week later two novels by Philip K. Dick in his open backpack, *The Man in the High Castle* and *The Three Stigmata of Palmer Eldritch*,

Dick having allegedly inspired Hubbard to devise his inter-galactic creed. There was something vaguely gothic about Dick, I thought, something sharp and in bad taste. He was paranoid yet flavorful, industrial strength.

We had a friend who'd grown up Mormon but re-nounced the faith at seventeen and ran away from home. He had lived in a basement in Oakland for a few years before going to college, then grad school. He had about twenty tattoos and a gold front tooth and loved antique furniture and cocaine. He and the man I was married to went through a period of binges, and somehow I associated it with Scientology. I'd listen to them discuss the unusual activities of the Angel Moroni and the irony of Abendsen's *The Grasshopper Lies Heavy* before we parted ways for the night, they to a fortress maintained by an eccentric dealer on Potrero Hill, I to my translations and, more impor-tantly, Craigslist.

There were two main things I was doing during the time I was not working at the temp agency, or sleeping, or eat-ing, or experiencing married sex, and these were: (1) trans-lating French Symbolist poetry, and (2) trawling Craigslist for employment. Specifically, I was interested in Stéphane Mallarmé, whom I considered glamorous as well as diffi-cult. Anyway, it was something I could talk about in mixed company. It was something that got people to leave me alone. "She's translating Mallarmé," the man I was married to said.

After this, I was left to my own devices and at liberty to navigate over to some listings.

When the American poet Frank O'Hara was pretty young, he made a translation of Mallarmé's poem, "Un coup de dés." It was something I liked to look at. I could contemplate the nature of fame. This was, by the way, before *Meditations in an Emergency* appeared in a scene in *Mad Men* and became, if briefly, a bestseller. O'Hara was one of the few poets the man I was married to had read, and he seemed to have romantic feelings for him. There was, leaning in an alcove near the entrance to our apartment, a bent postcard featuring a black-and-white photo of O'Hara: one of the only decorative additions to the place not made by me.

The man I was married to returned catatonic from his excursions with the ex-Mormon. He tapped his fingertips against his thumb in his sleep and ground his teeth.

I got out of bed. It was 2:35 a.m.

Beside my computer sat O'Hara's *Early Writing*. I admit there's a way I look a little like him; we have the same sad eyes. His translation begins, "A THROW OF THE DICE Even when thrown in eternal circumstances in the midst of a wreck BE It that the abysm whitened displays furious. . . ."

"'*Abysm*,'" I thought.

But I was only pretending to think about literature. I was on Craigslist and responding to an ad.

I wrote:

To Whom It May Concern,

I am a recent graduate of ____ University
(20__) and the University of _____ (20__)
who would love to craft some gripping, sen-
timental, and definitely erotic diary entries
for you. Please find a resume and several
recent movie reviews (www.flashfilm.com)
attached.

Thanks!

The next day I went to work and in the evening there
came a reply:

Hello

Thank you for your interest in our little
project. We are developing a small artistic
website where we shoot some erotic pictures
and erotic videos of a few girls. Each girl
has 5 or 6 photo shoots with some video
and an interview. We need to create a diary
for a few of them. This diary would consist
of 2 parts:

1. Actual blog (e.g. day 1 ... day 2 ... etc. . . .). Some days should have some connection to the photo shoots, but generally it's a very creative job. The only other condition is that there should be quite a bit of erotic content.

2. Also all the photos (and some of them could be repetitive) need some description. However, you can be creative here as well. Your description doesn't necessarily need to describe the picture . . . (e.g. if a girl drinks coffee you might right something about her memories of the past, if she kisses you can talk about texture of her lips etc . . . etc. . . .).

The total work is about 10 pages (up or down 1 or 2). Total pay for one diary is around $100.

Website is www.fotoconfessions.com

login: confessor
pwd: first

(it's operating only partially at this point but you'll get the general concept, take a look at the timeline on top of the page that allows you to go over to different entries. Also it's better to use explorer than firefox) Most of the girls need a diary. Please write back if you are interested.

Sincerely,
Lev

I held my breath. I had that feeling I had so often had in high school, as of a tracking shot.

Dear Lev, I began typing.

"I want," I thought that night, "to be free. But freedom is an intellectual demand and, as such, has nothing to do with pleasure." Far, far below, there was some sort of silvery substance. I could see it glittering there. Truthful, perhaps. Perhaps eternal.

I was not a man.

When I was with the man I was married to, I sometimes wanted him to stop.

"Don't come," he would tell me.

Pleasure was a tiny wall in the void, yet the void inhabited it.

In the midst of an unspeakable orgasm, I felt panic, then what I believed was the nearness of god.

I sometimes wondered what Mallarmé knew about

this. In 1874, Mallarmé had pseudonymously written all the articles for eight issues of a women's fashion magazine called *La Dernière mode* (*The Latest Fashion*). He became a variety of fictional authors of occasional prose, some male, some not. He was, among others, a Marguerite de Ponty, a Miss Satin, someone named "Ix," and Le Chef de bouche chez Brébant. These endeavors seemed completely ecstatic.

I was still writing to Lev. It was very late. I could only manage a single sentence: *Please let me know how I can get started.*

The man I was married to was sometimes in a sort of trance, and I did not understand, at the time, that such trances are given to people by their families.

I remember sitting with him in traffic, as a spell of rage overcame me. There was furniture tied to the roof. I was driving and could not speak.

The rage was dense and specific and had a syntax. The rage said, "Your life has no ceiling and no walls and no floor."

What I interpreted this to mean was that my life might not be my life. I might have wandered into someone else's story and was now failing to cease residing there. Every day, when I woke up, I failed. It was hard to understand how one could live a life that was not one's own without having any intention to do so, but here I was, letting such things come to pass.

In traffic, in the car, in one of his trances, furniture tied to the roof, the man I was married to observed my rage. He observed my inability to speak.

"What are you thinking?" he wanted to know.

I could not speak.

"You can't speak," he said, smiling. "You can't even talk right now."

Traffic loosened and I navigated to a parking spot.

You aren't supposed to talk about these things, the various ways he impaled me, the stars I saw.

There was a soft part to this, and there was something else.

I received a reply from Lev:

> Please take a girl named Alyssa and do 1/2 page of a diary and 3-4 captions under the pictures. Send it to me and we'll get started.

> Thank you

I did not talk about this with anyone. I felt a brief joy. In the morning, I went to work.

At work, the Australian was massive and upsettingly well formed. He was a terrible person and seemed to like walking past my desk. It was a common route for just about everyone and he needed no excuse.

"How's the weather?"

This was funny because I had no access to windows.

Later on, retrieving files from the bottom of some complex cabinet, bent over, I was approached by a more seasoned member of the staff, someone high up in billing. "That's quite a system you've got there," he told me, a reference, one could suppose, to the administrative code of colors and endless number chains with which the folders that were my domain were labeled.

I could not speak. But then I told him, "Yes. Yes, it is." And rose to face him.

Mallarmé loved foam. He loved something about the sea, the way it hisses in retreat, the way it is a glossy sheet of numbers, constantly multiplying and taking roots and falling into the pit of itself.

People seem to think that the shipwreck is the thing, but that's just wishful thinking. The shipwreck is something like a statue; it's not anything, but it can trick us. If Mallarmé had lived during the golden age of installation art (which, by the way, is ongoing), he might have built some sort of room. The shipwreck is a prop, an echo, a decoration from a long-ago-concluded party. We don't know it's not an origin. We don't know it's not what happened. We keep it as a sign or proof. We set it as a seal upon our foreheads and go on living.

The man I was married to and I went for walks along the Pacific.

No one could say our relationship was devoid of fantasy.

He liked to tell me about the activities of the ex-Mormon. He was learning a lot during their narcotic nights. They'd get as high as humanly possible, then go to a park to break things and talk.

The ex-Mormon was apparently footing the bill. The man I was married to explained that the ex-Mormon was extremely canny. He wasn't an average person and had long ago figured this out about himself. The ex-Mormon was OK with this. He did not force himself to conform.

The man I was married to examined a pair of flat stones. He made them click and skipped one.

"He's 'gay for pay,'" the man I was married to said. He described a scene in a recent pornographic video the ex-Mormon had been featured in, in which the ex-Mormon was slung up in a swing. Everyone was dressed as a clown. The ex-Mormon made $5,000.

"The great thing is, you can't see his face. With the makeup. It's this crazy niche."

The man I was married to continued to skip stones. "Maybe you should try it," he said.

It was the close of a warm day in early October. The sun was doing flattering things to the earth and air.

I was thinking about how there are so many shipwrecks in poetry, and I was also thinking about how Frank O'Hara died on a beach, hit by a dune buggy. It's a death that seems so wanton, so flimsy, like it has to be a suicide. O'Hara didn't die right away. He was young, forty. He died later, of injuries.

I realized, suddenly, that the ex-Mormon was a handsome man. He wasn't a bone-snapping killer like the Australian, but he, too, was attractive.

I wrote to Lev:

Hi Lev,

Here are captions for the spread that begins, "I am sleeping":

Line 1. Mmm. Such a beautiful dream, I'm in a grove of banana trees!

Line 2. Oh well, there's the alarm! Guess I'm just going to have to find a way to make that dream a reality. Wow, feel a little sore from

yesterday. Just thinking of how tight Bobby
pulled those straps . . .

Line 3. Just wish I had someone here. Someone like you. Who knows exactly what I like
and how to give it to me.

#

I am not sure what 1/2 page signifies, re:
diary, so will give you ~100wrds and hope
that's what you had in mind:

I was trying to get in touch with Bobby all
day. I have no idea where he was. It started
to get late. I was so lonely that I got dressed
up in my silky corset and lace-up boots. But
I didn't want to be blindfolded, and you can
guess why: I went into the bathroom and put
one foot up on the edge of the sink, imagining Bobby was there watching me. I got so
hot that I went over to the bed to finish myself off. That's when the doorbell rang. You
can guess who it was. I was so happy!

Best,

Soon my parents came to visit. Their take on my life with the man I was married to seemed to boil down to a single question: "Why are you poor?"

They took us out to lunch at the most expensive restaurant they could find, where my father insulted the waiter. The napkins had a very high thread count. I kneaded mine below the table. With my right hand I stirred some bisque.

The man I was married to chuckled politely.

My father glanced at a woman passing through another room. "Is that dress rubber?" he wondered, in slow and casual tones.

The man I was married to dutifully transferred his eyes to the mark.

I could not speak.

The woman was wearing a cotton shift.

A pit had opened. Everywhere was iridescent. The pit continued to sink, mechanized and sure.

"What's wrong?" asked my mother, somewhere.

It was magic.

The pit trembled. I could hear but could not move.

My mother brought the point of her napkin to her lips.

"How could he say that?" I managed, on a breath.

"What did I say?" my father bellowed. He was addressing my mother, who was patting him. "I asked a question about a dress!"

"Relax," stage-whispered the man I was married to. He put my spoon back into my hand.

I would go sometimes to the twenty-four-hour donut shop on the hill above our apartment. It wasn't a fancy place, but the Boston Creams were good and it had seating. It was owned by a family who didn't seem optimistic about the state of the world, but they knew a lot of the people who came in and maintained a supportive tone. It was a place where I could go to mourn.

I sat along one of the windows, at a narrow counter. I always had black tea with milk along with my Boston Cream, which I cut into small pieces with a plastic knife in a futile attempt to make it less caloric.

It was usually the same man or his precocious daughter who helped me. They didn't comment on my repeat visits.

I'd sit along the window and stare at words arranged by Mallarmé. I wrote: Like listening to Genesis read in reverse. Always this sense, Mallarmé's sentences are occurring in reverse. I kept looking at a certain set of lines: "naufrage cela / direct de l'homme / sans nef." I wrote: That shipwreck of the man directly without a ship. I put a pair of parentheses around "directly." I erased the parentheses.

Outside, a tram rumbled by, taking people somewhere with mystifying inefficiency.

One evening the man at the donut shop asked, "How old are you?"

I said, because I really wanted to know, "How old do you think I am?"

"You're twenty-five," said the man.

"You're right," said I.

"Well, have a good night," he told me.

I walked back down the hill, revising my mental list of shipwrecks in poetry.

Lev said:

> I like what you wrote. So, let's start with Alyssa.
>
> To recap: About 7 pages of diary (up or down a bit is ok.) We measure page in a standard way. Then captions.
>
> Please write 3-4 lines per row of photos. e.g. [1 row: It was so nice to see Bobby . . .] Then second row etc. . . .
>
> We'll end up with plus or minus three pages.

Consider yourself hired for Alyssa's diary. If
all is well, we'll hire you for the next one.

If you have questions you can reach me by
415.____.____

Here are the shipwrecks I know of in poetry:
Odysseus of course had difficulties sailing, as did the
apostle Paul, who was shipwrecked four times. John Milton
had a good friend named Edward King who died in waters
near Wales in the first half of the seventeenth century, and
this event inspired "Lycidas," a poem with the strange for-
mulation, "wat'ry floor." Sickly John Keats was done in by a
boat trip and his friend Shelley, who later drowned in a sailing mishap, memorialized him in "Adonais." Emily Dickin-
son had a floor, too: "If my Bark sink / 'Tis to another sea — /
Mortality's Ground Floor / Is Immortality —" Gerard Man-
ley Hopkins wrote "The Wreck of the Deutschland," a poem
about the unthinkable and how it is somehow sanctioned by
god. And I am leaving out *The Tempest* by Shakespeare, although I am thinking, too, of Aimé Césaire's *Une Tempête*,
in which Prospero is at pains to explain to Miranda that
the storm and wreck they are observing are no more than a
play. The American poet and labor organizer George Oppen
wrote of "The unearthly bonds / Of the singular / Which is

the bright light of shipwreck," and another American, Hannah Weiner, said, "I am a complete wreck."

And there is Mallarmé.

At the temp agency there was a woman in her early thirties. She had ironed hair and wore a pantsuit with a seventies attitude although the pantsuit came from Ann Taylor. She was undeniably chic and had a good position and was married to someone very rich. She was interested that I, too, was married.

"Are you planning to have children?"

I said something about how I wasn't sure of anything yet, which she took to be an expression of appreciation for the corporate ladder. She began to reel off names of persons I would need to meet.

I waited for an opening. "Are you planning to have children?"

"Oh yes," she said. "We start this summer."

"How wonderful," I told her, feeling adult.

"Look at my ring," she offered, suddenly trusting me. "Isn't it amazing? It's Cartier. They only made like ten of them. It's brushed titanium with platinum and sapphire and black opal. I like it so much more than a single setting, and it's so unique. I was so, so touched when my husband suggested it."

"Wow," I said.

"Can I see yours?"

"It's just plain gold."

"Wow," she told me.

"I picked it out."

"Well," she said, handing it back, "I'm sure your husband loves you more than that."

I wrote to Lev:

> sorry this has taken me so long, it will usually only take me 24hrs to turn over an assignment of this length. please let me know about payment and if you have more diaries you need written.
>
> thanks!

#

1. Dear Diary, I woke up this morning and didn't know where I was. The first thing I noticed, though, was that I couldn't open my eyes. There was something heavy and kind of cool covering them. Probably a leather blindfold. Maybe it was weighted somehow, like there was metal inside it. I noticed also

that my wrists were a little tender (not to mention certain other parts, which I won't mention, because I'm sure you're thinking about them already). I moved my arms around experimentally. They were stretched away from my body, securely fastened by some type of leather cuff or straps to the posts of my bed. I wiggled. I could feel now that my legs were also restrained, in a predictable position, and that I was wearing a leather harness that cut into the skin at my hips, but not in a totally unpleasant way.

It was kind of hard to breathe. I lay there, pulling in short sips of air. I thought, and I don't quite know how to tell you this, that I could feel drops of water on my face and maybe on my chest and stomach. Then the water began to really fall. I don't know where it came from. It was warm and I felt myself being bathed but I had to struggle to get air. The water was everywhere, running over me, and then it stopped.

"Bobby?" I whispered.

"No," said a female voice. "This isn't Bobby."

2. I think I was hallucinating yesterday. Maybe dreaming. I don't know what it was. I woke up again, late, and there was nothing unusual going on. The only thing was, my hair was damp. I guess it could have been sweat.

I got up, feeling angry at Bobby. I wrote him an email telling him things were getting out of hand and I refused to see him that day or ever again. I know that sounds a little unfair—but I want Bobby to know, just in case he doesn't understand, that he can't just sneak up on me, psychologically speaking, without there being repercussions. I mean, my mind is my temple, and my experience with men has taught me that you have to make it a little hard for them! And in Bobby's case, well, you can guess . . . how I feel . . . The problem is, I might be an addict. But never mind all that, because I had an amazing adventure today.

I decided to treat myself to a movie in the afternoon. I worked out all morning and took a long hot shower. Then I put on moisturizer (almond butter, it's the only kind I'll use), slipped on one of my favorite panties (nothin' but string, baby!), and got into one of my velour lounge suits. I didn't wear a bra because, well, it was just one of those days—and I like the feeling of the material. Oh, and I wore lots of lip gloss.

The movie was this cheesy spy-thriller I've been wanting to see for a while; I guess I kind of have a thing for the lead actor (it's the way he's so good with his hands!). I was just starting to get bored when I noticed this cute boy sit down in my row two seats away from me. The theater was very dark, and there weren't too many other people there. I waited to see if he'd notice me, and when he did, I very slowly started sliding down the zipper on my top until it was down below my belly button. Then I slipped one hand in. Now I could tell I had his attention, so I put my hand in my pants. I was imagining what he would think about my underwear. I wished we were somewhere else. But I thought I'd settle for the here and now. I think he knew what I had in mind, because he got up and came over and sat next to me to help out.

3. I have basically forgiven Bobby. Tonight I let him take me out to dinner. It was a simple affair. I wore a new pantsuit with a corset-top that felt wonderfully tight. We ate at a small French restaurant, it had maybe 10 tables. I ordered oysters and roast chicken and then salad. Bobby just sat there watching me eat. He didn't even touch his wine. The whole time I felt he was looking at me in a new way, as if he had discovered he desired me differently since I'd told him about what I'd dreamed the other morning and how it had upset me so much I might never want to see him again. I was almost afraid of him. It was like he knew something about me that he'd never known before, and maybe it was something no one else had ever been able to discover. What could it be? I did not invite Bobby home with me. I am waiting until tomorrow to decide what to do.

4. Late last night I started missing Bobby, and I decided to make a little movie for him. I got the big mirror off of the wall in my bedroom and set it up on the floor with the camera resting on top. I decided this was going to be a movie all about my fears. I sat

down on the carpet in my underwear, with a box of matches. I turned on the camera and started taking off my bra and panties very slowly. Once I was naked, I lit a match. I just sat there, watching it burn down to my fingertips in the mirror. When it started to burn me, I looked at the image of myself. I watched myself wince and flinch. I made myself keep looking even though it hurt. There started to be this other part of me there, then, just as I knew there would. I could already feel myself starting to lose control. My hands were shaking, but I lit another match and held it. I was watching myself do this. I brought it down to my knee. But then I jumped up and shut the camera off and went and dropped the matches in the sink and turned the faucet on full blast.

5. I emailed the movie to Bobby. I think he liked it. He told me it was "deep." He's asked me if I will make another one for him or tell him more about my fantasies. I suddenly feel shy again, as if maybe I'm revealing too much about myself. I do have another fantasy to share with Bobby, but I'm not sure if I should. Here it is, Dear Diary. Maybe

you can help me decide what I should do. I want to be taking a shower, when Bobby suddenly enters my apartment and then the bathroom. He picks me up and carries me to my bed, where he blindfolds me, ties my hands, ties my ankles. And then he leaves. He just leaves me there. And I can't move. And when he leaves he locks the door. And then he goes and gets boards and nails them over the door. And then he goes and gets bricks and mortar and bricks over the wood. And then he goes and gets stucco and paint and makes a perfect wall. I can hear him working. And then there is silence and I cannot move and I feel the weight of the bricks on my face even though they're nowhere near me. They're so heavy and so cool weighing me down. And it hurts so much and is so peaceful, and during the hundreds of years that pass even Bobby dies and I am completely unknown . . .

6. I told Bobby about my new fantasy. I think it definitely excited him. He told me he would come over soon, so I'm just getting ready to see him. I put fresh sheets on the bed, and I've been ____ _____ __ _____.

I am so excited, I'm almost _____. It's all I can do not to _____ _____, but I want to wait for him to _____. I think I am going to wear a white dress in the shower so Bobby can tug on it and maybe it will be see-through and _____. Or maybe I'll wear this white ____ _____ _____ that doesn't have _____ where _____ should be. I should _____ my _____ _____. I'd like that. Well, I better get the water hot, I think Bobby will be here soon.

Lev replied instantly:

I don't think you mean "almond butter"

Second, I don't know what half this is, including the mad lib (?)

Give me a call please

I took off early on a Friday, the next day, so I could speak with Lev. I was mortified, but I did not know what else to do.

"Hi, may I please speak to Lev?"

"Yeah, here."

"Hi."

"Who's this?"

"It's, uh," I started to say.

"Oh," he said, "it's *you*. Writer girl."

I made a noise.

"Yeah, one second." Lev seemed to walk into another room. "Sorry, I'm in the studio. You should come down sometime."

I didn't say anything. I wasn't sure what a pornographer was supposed to sound like. Lev sounded brisk, lucid.

"OK," he announced, "I have officially entered the green room. Let me call this thing up." Time passed. "OK, looking at it. You have too much investment. That's what I think."

"Sure," I said.

"I like it in some ways. I won't lie."

I didn't say anything. I could tell that Lev was lean. He was not exactly short, but he wasn't tall, either. He was lean and had a simple countenance.

"Care less and be brutal. How does that sound?"

"Yes," I said.

"Yes? Yes is not an answer to my question." Lev was typing something. "Sorry, one second."

I waited.

"OK. I'm back. You understand what this is for? I'm not trying to be a fascist."

I didn't say anything.

"I would like it if this works. I would like it if it would work."

"I get it," I said.

"You were showing a lot of potential there. You have a nice light touch. But brutal, OK?"

"I want to try again."

Lev said, "There's a part of it you understand, right, where it's a game and it's something you can look at, but there's another part, too, where it's only happening. Do you understand?"

"Yes," I said.

"You can visit the past, but don't live there."

"Yes," I repeated, uncomprehending.

"I was hoping we could work together," Lev said.

Yes, I was thinking, no.

My face started shaking and I accidentally hung up.

The man I was married to got into an accident on his bicycle. He was coming to an intersection at the bottom of a hill. He went over his handlebars and flew onto the hood of someone's car. The driver gave him $700 to walk away. He came home to lie in bed with a fuchsia bruise hooked from his left nipple to the center of his back.

The bruise looked like a sickle or thin moon.

"Good job walking away," I said.

The man I was married to was munching some Bayer, flipping through a tabloid.

"Aaron is leaving," he said.

This was the ex-Mormon.

"He got a job and needs to relocate. He wants to try it for a year."

"Is this more acting?"

"No. It's more textbooks."

"Weird," I said.

"Not really. Some uncle set it up. I guess he's going back in the fold."

"Maybe they're running out of men."

"*Maybe*," said the man I was married to. I could tell his injury was bothering him. I sat on the edge of the bed, feeling some of his pain. If I shifted, it would hurt him, I could tell.

I shifted.

The man I was married to did not react.

The tabloid was between us, and the man I was married to turned a page.

BIG CUTS FOR WEALTHY, the tabloid said.

I shifted again.

That night we went out with the ex-Mormon to celebrate his new future. The ex-Mormon's hair was so light it was white in the bar. He was a large, freckled cat. His eyes were pale green, nearly yellow. He was the product of inbreeding, heavy and thin at once, pale and dark, canny and naïve. I could tell there was something about humanity that he had come to understand, and perhaps accept, that I never would, and I think this made me angrier.

I observed the ex-Mormon, wrapped in his superior narrative, undeniable in spite of his ex-ness. Maybe even the apostates got to go to a private planet with a low-melanin female janitorial staff, after death.

The man I was married to was taking an extra-long time in the bathroom, probably because of the injury, but who could say for sure.

I entered into a fresh Maker's Mark, noting that my tab now constituted a full ninety minutes of my employed labor.

"It's a job," the ex-Mormon said, "but I'm planning to like it."

I realized that he had been talking to me for a little while now about his forthcoming rebirth into the middle class. I hadn't been listening to him because there was something pounding in my ears. It was the voice I could always hear, once I got wasted.

The Mormon would marry someday and have children, and he knew it. The man I was married to would marry again someday and have children, and he knew it, too. But what was I going to do?

It seemed not to be enough for me, I realized, that possibly I was free, forgetting for a moment about the machinations of capital. I was free and could act, and from my actions would be composed an event. And out of a single event, and another event, would be composed yet another event, which was a story.

But beneath these facts, which I could say to myself and hear myself say, and even understand as a style of logic, there was something else.

If I could drink another drink, maybe I could listen to this thing. This was the thing where a garland of flowers bursts apart into a ring of porpoises. Beads of foam act as a kind of prism. It can't be undone but it is being undone right now. The floor of time drops down, releasing a cloud of sand, and from out of the shipwreck, tragic but below us, harmony reconstitutes itself.

Tomorrow I would be walking up that hill again, soon, because a throw of the dice will never abolish chance.

Cosmogony

A few years ago a friend of mine married a demon. There was a liberal in the White House then and everyone was feeling pretty sanguine.

The demon's name was Fulmious Mannerhorn Patterlully, and he was approximately 200,001 years old. His legs were blue; his eyes were yellow; he had to gnaw at his own fingernails all day to keep them a reasonable length. He did not wear pants with notable frequency. He was intelligent, gregarious, undying.

My friend was twenty-eight. She was a human girl.

We'd always known about demons. They were the necessary, baleful entities that stood on the porches of history, holding up the roofs of civilization with their knotted backs. They were the reason that the past was visible to us at all.

People kept complimenting my friend on her choice of partner—and I know you get it, too. Although people did not say so in so many words, what they meant was that my friend now partook of the powers of the demon FMP without having to experience any of the drawbacks associated with actual demonhood. The demon FMP could (and, presumably, would) share with my friend his occult understanding of the stock market, his ability to produce fire on demand, his talent for translating himself into a fine mist. He liked to hang, shimmering, from the ceilings of crowded subways, for example. He enjoyed magnetizing coins and possessing small dogs, speaking to us in funny voices through their squinty wet faces. He was an expert in the objectification of souls and had a long-standing social network.

And this was good for my friend. But the demon FMP alone experienced that terrible period in April when demons undergo new growth in their horns, not to mention the insidious agony that comes of eternal life.

My friend seemed to understand the trade-offs, as well as society's position on the matter. She took it all in stride. "I know he's an infernal demiurge, but he's actually just a nice guy."

Everyone grinned hard.

My friend wasn't talking to us, anyway. She was describing her own happiness, which had its limits. We wanted to believe that she knew more than we did, but, in truth, even my friend did not know where things were going to go.

Now, my friend had mentioned to me, at some point during the time when she was engaged to the venerable FMP but not yet married, that there is a little-known fact about demons, which is that they have two different names, or sets of names, given FMP's tripart moniker. There is the name by which they are known to humans, and the one by which they are known among themselves. My friend said that at some point during a certain particularly poignant night of passion and spooning, the demon FMP had let slip the fact of the existence of his other name, his real name, the name by which he was known among demons.

"It must be hard," I said, "going all those millennia."

She was reserved. "I'm not his first human, you know."

I was doing my best not to imagine whatever it was that transpired between my friend and her supernatural other on the carnal plane. "So, what is it?"

"You mean, his *real name*?"

I nodded.

My friend seemed to contemplate my lack of inhibition. It wasn't the same thing as rudeness, and I think that she was wondering if one day this lack of tact would destroy me—or if, because of it, I was destined to live an unusual life.

I kept going. I said, "Wasn't I there that night you recited Shakespeare to Thom Velez in the motel hot tub? Didn't I hold your hair until 9 a.m.?"

My friend blushed. I could tell she loved me.

"Won't I be there," I pursued, "after *everything*, even when he's gone?"

"But you realize"—my friend was daintily reaching for her phone—"that he's never going to, um, your euphemism, 'be gone'?"

My friend thumbed through something or other.

"I'll die before him," my friend continued, gazing into her iPhone 8, which was encased in a piece of plastic designed to resemble marble. "You know?"

So she never did tell me her fiancé's demon name.

But I still found out. I'm sure you understand: I always do.

It was after their wedding. I was in the supermarket, the one at the corner of _____ and _____, assessing the rows of cherry tomatoes. I lifted multiple pints, gazed up into their see-through bottoms searching for fuzz. And there, suddenly, FMP was. I saw him out of the corner of my eye; it was the blueness of his legs, which appeared weirdly white or violet in the afternoon light. He was tearing pieces off a glistening danish, popping them into his maw as he engaged a young artist whom I recognized as the subject of a recent *Artforum* pick in a lazy chat pertaining to the shop and, one had to assume, eternal damnation.

FMP was staring right at me.

I stared right back.

I knew it was weird but I couldn't help myself. I directed my gaze firmly and robustly back to the bottom of the tomato container I was holding up. I knew well it was the wrong thing to do. An ambitious parent had long ago instructed me, specifically and in detail, never to look a demon in their eyes and look away again without acknowledging the encounter. It was a gross offense. But this was exactly what I had done. FMP had seen me, and I had seen his yellow eyes that basked calmly and yellow-ly in their furred sockets. I recalled that line of Edgar Allan Poe's: "And his eyes have all the seeming of a demon's that is dreaming." It's from "The Raven," something I once memorized in an institutional context. I often remark to myself regarding Poe's dorky specificity: His eyes (the raven's) have the appearance of a demon's (eyes!), and, meanwhile, the demon, and not his eyes, is dreaming. . . . Because grammar and syntax are real! Life is not all about magic and deities, even if it sometimes seems like it is, whether due to one's liquid laudanum habit (have a nice jarful on your afternoon stroll and get ready to unleash some neo-gothic lyrics!) or one's best friend's marriage to a minion of Dis. Edgar Allan Poe, for one, understood that you *do* need to know whether it's the demon who's dreaming or just its eyes. He would never have been so stupid as to do what I just did.

Anyway, there I was staring into the glossy redness of miniature tomatoes, themselves not unlike a bunch of disembodied eyes, when I smelled FMP's sulfurous approach.

"Well, hello," said he.

I laughed weakly. "Just researching the ways of very small nightshades!"

FMP reacted with solemnity. "Of course." It was always difficult to ascertain if he might be joking, and at this moment the ambiguity was daunting, slimy. "I thought I'd say 'hi.'" FMP smiled, releasing a fascinating, hideous stench from between his peg-like teeth. "By the way, it's come to my attention that there was something you wanted to *know*."

I was sure I did not know what he meant.

"About *me*? Or have you forgotten so soon? I was extremely touched that you were interested in my True Name." The way he said it, it had to be capitalized.

"Um, not sure?"

"Oh no. You're sure, you shallow wretch. Even if I were not the life partner of a being with whom you are bonded through shared trauma, nearly identical socioeconomic standing, and level of physical attractiveness, as well as geographic proximity, I'd still know. It was obvious in your desperate attempt to avoid this very encounter. You're a coward," FMP told me. "Yet it alleviates the torment of my archaic burden somewhat to watch you squirm. Thank you for that. I like your superficially independent, spineless style, you immature female specimen," and here he also reeled off my credit score, Social Security number, number of porcelain vs. gold tooth fillings, and the date on which I was currently scheduled to die.

It's not, by the way, like this was an anomalous encounter with FMP. He was constantly like this, reminding you of your mortality plus vulnerability to identity theft. A lot of people seemed to find this charming, a cool party trick, but it had occurred to me that this behavior must have been going on with him for centuries if not geologic eras, and I didn't find FMP all that original, even in his omniscience.

"Right again," said I.

FMP glittered with malice. All his hairs stuck out. He was having a great time. "I know," he let me know, "that you want what's mine."

I shrugged but had to go fondle some nearby fennel in order to hide the trembling in my hands.

"I'm going to tell you my True Name," FMP whisper-shouted. "Then you will know it!" It was all extremely mechanical and ancient. It was the best and the most unpleasant thing. It is such an event to speak with a demon! "My True Name," FMP hissed across a heap of broccoli rabe, "is 27."

"Wait," I said, "*what*?"

"Twenty-seven," FMP repeated.

"As in, the number?"

FMP looked annoyed. "No, it just sounds like that."

I didn't know what to say. "Twenty-seven?" I repeated.

FMP, a.k.a. 27, was glancing around the store. He seemed concerned that he had made a mistake.

"27," I muttered to myself. "27." I couldn't believe it. I think I must have wandered unceremoniously off, because the next thing I can remember I was standing on the sidewalk.

And, just to say, if you thought my encounter with FMP/27 was startling, which, granted, it was, I don't quite know how to explain the subsequent scenario.

It was how *he* looked, because that's always part of it. But that wasn't all. There was also this quality about him, a kind of un-believability, and I think I can point to it in this moment, when it was still fresh. I was probably squinting into a device, trying to refresh my email.

"Hi," he said. "Sorry to bother you. Were you just in the market over there?" Note that he did not say "supermarket," just "market." Note also that he was an otherworldly being. Now that he was present, the light seemed not to originate in the sky but rather from somewhere on the inside of him. "I'm so sorry," he said again. "Many apologies." It's impossible to describe his voice. It was soft, delicately wilted, but also it was like the mighty crash of apocalyptic hailstorms, jet engines, stampeding mares.

I nodded. Probably I made one of those incoherent noises of assent that have become so popular in postwar America. "Yeah," I said. "Unhuhn. Mmhmm. Heh!" I was a moron, typical of my time.

The being smiled. "I thought it was you. I'd like to speak

with you. I'd like to know you." Please note how this was extremely direct. He was tactless, just like me.

Maybe I had the wherewithal to reply in words. I dearly hope I did. At any rate, somehow it came to pass that a week later we were having coffee.

And isn't it clear by now? He was the exact opposite and equal of FMP/27. Oh, the symmetry! Oh dear god! Oh how fearful! How precise! He was an actual *angel*, and his name was Eric.

Eric was subtle at first. To be fair, we did establish during our second encounter that I was an acquaintance, if not quite ally, of FMP. Eric built that fact out like a custom cabana, a dell we could retire to should we run out of things to say. And it was true that in the beginning Eric did not push me. This was likely much of the secret to his success, that he did a host of other things but he did not push. I do sometimes wonder: Which parts of what occurred were due to Eric's immutable role within the cosmos, and which had to do with something similar to free will, perhaps the portion of it belonging to me, a minor anthropomorphic pleat in the fabric of eternity? Was any of it, I keep asking myself, "for" me, a human girl?

I, for my part, was twenty-nine and, like everyone else these days, a product of the Enlightenment. I believed that dating (along with everything else) occurred in a wide, wide, secular zone. Sure, there might be devils and angels and true believers, but what did that really matter, now that we had the news? Everything was basically all about information:

who possessed it, who didn't. So, there might be some level at which Eric could bring about my salvation, but that was just one piece of the puzzle, and I was actually more interested in whether he might be privy to anything proprietary regarding me or relevant others: sensitive thoughts, secrets, insecurities, lusts.

The idea of the network, as described in Gottfried Leibniz's 1714 tract, *La Monadologie*, pretty much the number-one guide to dating ever in the history of the West, furnishes a useful description:

To the extent that I comprehend it, in Leibniz's conception the world is made up of various shiny, translucent cells ("monads"), and each of these cells can perceive other cells, its own unique identity being constituted by its various perceptions of these infinitely various others. If any one monad depends on something external to itself, then it depends on *others*—an infinite number of them, and not just *an other*, since it is only by virtue of the many, the perceptions they provide, that there is such a thing as a *one*.

If you're with me so far, let's make an inference. I think it might be interesting to ask what the responsibility of one monad is to another. I think we can safely say they owe each other everything and also nothing. For what can be the meaning of a pair, a couple, in a structural environment such as this—I mean, for just two monads, given the propensity to reflect and just, like, go on reflecting? What are they to each other?

You can imagine that, if it works for monads that they get their identity by having a unique perspective on all other monads, then if you take two of them and sequester them somewhere (say, Eric's so-so apartment) so that they only have each other to work with, the effects are crazy. Each of these two monads, now isolated as a couple, can only take its respective identity from reflecting the other. If we slow the process down so that we can look at it step by step, in time, we see something like, monad A reflects monad B, and vice versa (they each become the other, $A \rightarrow B^R$, $B \rightarrow A^R$). In step 2, they then each reflect themselves *as the other,* so if monad A has already become B^R and B has become A^R, then in the second glance they are $B^R \rightarrow A^{RR}$ and $A^R \rightarrow B^{RR}$. This can go on for a very long time.

While I'm not saying that this is really what happens in romantic relationships, it might be what people have a tendency to think is going on. This is also how they decide who is the bad person in the relationship, and who is the good. Of course, given the monadical model, they're basically the same person, if not entirely composed of each other. However, few couples recognize this simple point. There's always one person who wants to feel worse about themself, and this, my secular Enlightenment-inheriting friends, makes all the difference.

But Eric and I didn't talk about ethics or psychology or the structure of the cosmos. He was an angel and thus already good.

I was, as noted, but a human girl.

Eric rented a junior one-bedroom. And indeed it was so-so, but it overlooked a park where some of the few birds that continue to inhabit New York City sang. I remember the first time that I learned that the etymology of "angel" brings us to a Greek word for messenger, go-between. It makes sense. "Demon" is more insoluble. It was inherited whole-sale and just means demon, although without some of the negative connotation. I often wondered if Eric had looked these histories up, too, or if he knew what these terms meant innately, without research.

Eric had a job. By this I mean he went to work every day at a small IT company with an office overlooking the Holland Tunnel. I think this was part of the reason people were so much bigger on the sort of relationship my friend and FMP had. FMP was completely consumed by his role as a tempter of souls and artisan of fate. He was vaguely famous and didn't require a day job. I'm not trying to say that, as an angel, Eric was some kind of idealist—it's just not entirely clear what he and his team were trying to do.

Eric bought all his clothes from AmazonBasics. He was often online. Far from being tactless, it turned out that he did not speak very much at all. He went down to the park. He waited.

I pondered Eric's muscular, winged form. It was often walking away from me. He was a sort of intergalactic male model, I thought: quiet, strong, chrononautic.

To return for a moment to the shape of the world: in an early essay, "On Language as Such and on the Language of Man," the twentieth-century critic and mystic Walter Benjamin worries about human speech. He tells us, on the one hand, that "Every expression of human mental life can be understood as a kind of language," and, on the other, sighs, "Speechlessness: that is the great sorrow of nature. . . ." In Benjamin's account, nature mourns the inadequacy of human speech, its petty enumerative names. Speechless herself, nature receives and believes the story of the creative word of Genesis, turning a melancholy face toward mankind, who can only supply a "hundred languages . . . in which [the] name has already withered, yet which, according to God's pronouncement, have knowledge of things." Setting aside some aspects of this description that could trouble those of us who accept the tidings of science, I found myself thinking a lot about this notion, in those days of Eric, who was so graceful and perfect and taciturn. In other words, I found myself thinking about how everything regarding human systems for organizing the world is basically fallen and repetitious. This was weird for a number of reasons but primarily it was weird because, you know, the Enlightenment! We're not supposed to have these sorts of thoughts anymore.

Also we're all supposed to be OK with the notion that we can't fully know one another. I think about it like this: Leibniz says that the irony of being human is that you're just like everyone else. You have all the same stuff everyone else has, just in a different order. The reason it is in a different order is that you have some sort of discrete origin, you were born in a time and place, and that, in combination with your embedding among various discrete others/quanta, is what makes you you. This difference is completely arbitrary and the system is designed in this completely infuriating way that makes it impossible to know about it—which is to say, your difference—as a kind of content. Which is why medieval Europeans all look like dolls in their paintings. There wasn't anything unknowable about them. They were the puppets of god, and they didn't have psychology or newspapers.

However, one of the few interesting things about being a woman is maybe the Enlightenment didn't happen for you. Like, you know how to speak and read and participate in democracy, but maybe you aren't really any better off. There are analogies between being female and being left-handed, I think, or being an animal. While I was with Eric, I thought a lot about the limits of psychology—or, as I privately referred to it now, "monad chatter." Monad chatter is going on in the world and meanwhile the world sits glumly by. We monads cannot get over the fact that we can't fully know one another. We'll surveil each other until the cows come home and pretend it's for marketing or science or spy craft. But really all this data is just a burnt offering to a god who withdrew long ago, leaving us the mute earth and also the vestiges of good and evil. And I guess we're free to care about, or even date, these vestiges, if we so choose.

As time went on, things were more and more placid and even quieter, but on occasion I caught Eric looking at me in a certain way. It was hard to say what sort of way this was because, having managed to fall deeply in love with him, I was more than a little confused.

"He's not the marrying kind," my friend said. "He dresses like an undercover cop."

I assumed she was jealous or in some other way annoyed by my righteous mode of affiliating myself with the deific. Also, I had begun to consider her immoral. Why was she consorting with a demon when we all knew demons were the one thing rendering this perfect universe impure?

My friend, meanwhile, was looking up at me with a mixture of recognition and pity. "So I guess you're going to play this one out to the bitter end?"

"I guess so!" I yelped, pitying her right back.

When I got home from the latest New American Restaurant that evening, home now being Eric's so-so apartment where I kept a small pile of belongings neatly stowed in discarded Prime packaging, Eric was hunched at his desk. He was filling out some sort of online form that he minimized as soon as I walked in.

"Hey you!" he said.

"Hi there." I hopped over and stroked one of his translucent feathers. I felt the usual electric charge and began drooling. I wondered if he felt like going to bed.

"In a minute. I was just thinking. Remember that day, when we first met?"

I said something about how could I forget but he ignored me. I think, anyway, that it was a rhetorical question.

"You were in the market that day. Do you remember?"

This was not a rhetorical question. I nodded.

"You spoke to someone there. That person is important to me." Eric paused. "For my work. I mean, my *real* work. Do you remember?"

I nodded again.

"And who was that?"

"FMP."

"Yes and no," said the angel, his eyes vibrating softly. "What was his *real* name?"

Of course, all is fair in love and war but you don't know how fair it really is until you become intimate with a being who looks pretty much exactly like a human but is not a human at all. At this point, I would not have denied Eric anything. I couldn't have. He represented my salvation. He explained things. I don't mean, by the way, that he explained things *to* me, with his voice and words and so forth. I mean, he, his presence, explained everything that had happened. He explained why I had had to go through what I'd gone through, all the years of isolation, my strange inability to find individuals to whom I could relate. My bizarre talk-ativeness. This had all happened because he was here. And now he just was.

I said, "Oh, you mean his *real* name," as if I knew exactly what was going down, as if I had known all along and was even waiting for this moment. "I'm surprised you never asked! It's 27, of course." I was terrified but manifested confidence. I put my hands on my hips. I stared bravely into the abyss that was opening up around me.

Eric raised an eyebrow. "Thanks," he muttered, stepping out an open window. He was evidently going to work.

I never saw Eric again. And I never saw my friend again, either. FMP, I heard, was reduced to a coal briquette. All in all, given these atypical goings-on, it's been a strange spring. I've realized how little I know of the ways of the world, how much there is that has come before. Yet I feel that I have made a lot of progress, that I'm slowly comprehending more. I marvel, and I try to be tough. I try to grow. I still have Eric's so-so apartment, by the way, and sometimes I go for walks in the park. There really is something lovely, something touching about survival.

On that last point, a few final remarks. Even more recently, over the past few days, maybe the last week and a half, I've been experiencing these headaches. They're brief, but when they strike they're like nothing you've ever known, believe you me. They feel like something stiff and sharp is trying to bore its way *out* of your skull.

It's made me start thinking more carefully about demons. You do see them now and then, doubled over in some discreet location, given the month. I think, too, as it can't be avoided, about Eric, an angel, whom I've come to regard less as a self-idealizing sociopath than a sort of amphibian, although he definitely put one over on me.

I've been told by numerous acquaintances that I'm looking pretty good. Their softballs re: breakup weight loss sail over my head. Sometimes it's because I'm dealing with a migraine, but at other times it's because I'm lost in thought.

Immortals, I'm thinking, they're just like us.

Recognition of This World
Is Not the Invention of It

The first time I understood the way things work, I was in control. My control was going to be short-lived, which was part of the way things work and how I started to know it. I stumbled guilelessly into this understanding, and I've never forgotten it, in no small measure because of what happened next.

What happened next I will explain in a moment. It was night. I was seated in a circle with ten or so other people. We were outdoors. At the center of our circle was a campfire, and at the center of this campfire was the invisible point in space and time at which our respective gazes met. At this point, bobbing and weaving among white-pink flames and sometimes passing out of view, something was taking place, was being exchanged. Let us call this process of exchange *D*. We can then represent *D* through the following equation, given what we know of the other variables involved:

$$D = p(g)$$

... where the small *p* is the number of persons implicated, with *g* standing for the *gaze sum average*, the calculation of which, along with related contingencies, we have already discussed in the precedent chapter. As was also intimated there, *D* is, in any given instance, affected by ancestry as well as the styles of ignorance, repression, passion, and fear tolerated by a given subject at a given moment in the subject's mortal trajectory. Therefore, in order to render *D* in non-ideal circumstances, i.e., outside the lab, we need to subtract the *blind-spot quantum*, *b*, from the equation, so that:

$$D - b = p(g), \text{ and, therefore, } g = (D - b)/p$$

This was what I wanted to know. *g. g!* Everything was *g*. I wanted to know how my looking contributed to my own agency, which was the meaning of this sacred variable, *g*. I wanted to know if what *I saw* was more or less than the average, if my *g* was a normal one, because, to be perfectly frank with you, I seemed to be seeing quite a lot in those days, possibly too much.

For example, on this particular night at this particular gathering (office workers pried loose from their urban setting and reassembled in bucolic surrounds), I was playing a game. Or, rather, *we* were playing a game, a sort of trust-building exercise which had the surprising, given the stated intent, name of Murder.

Murder is, as I found out that night, fairly well known. Just because I hadn't played it before and did not understand the rules did not mean that others were by any means unfamiliar. There were, in fact, several versions or strains or modes of Murder: San Francisco Style, Toronto Rules, and, finally, Bloody Boots, the last of which is a faster-paced technique of play. Everyone tried to be patient as various experts among us weighed in. Everyone poured more whiskey or Fernet into their cups of melted ice cream and cake fragments and smoked; everyone, that is, save Keith, who was nursing a flavored Pellegrino.

Keith was sort of my boss, but more on this later. Keith wore long shorts and crossed his excellent legs. He sat shyly in the darkness. Or perhaps he sat immorally. I was very drunk and very high and could not tell.

I was, however, not so drunk nor so high that I could not muster up the desire to win. I wasn't sure what it was to win at Murder, but I was determined to be the person who did win. I wanted to dominate, to play Murder as it had never before been played.

To this end, I began creating in myself a space of resolve. I used to have an equation that represented the dynamics of what went on in this space, but by this point in time I'd pretty much abandoned all attempts to quantify it. The reason that I had abandoned this descriptive project was that my representations of what was taking place inside me in no way corresponded to what was happening outside, in the world. Just when I thought I'd figured out how to square a given circle, it would turn out that the terms of engagement were being rewritten, I'd missed some key detail, I was ineffective, overambitious, and wrong. I still had the ability to create my space of resolve and I still did stuff with it, it just wasn't all that clear why. But I was sauced, as I said, and high, and so I began freely scheming.

The way that our game of Murder was shaping up was, insofar as I understand things, pretty much the norm. One person, Gary, a junior designer and a member of the Murder cognoscenti among us, was acting as Narrator. And, oh yes, the murderer had already been selected through a secret, random process that I do not recall. (Were slips of paper handed out?)

"It is night," intoned the narrator, which was doubly true. He meant that we should close our eyes.

And this was where it began for me, my understanding of the way things work, because although I comprehended the rules of the game, and although I was the sort of person who liked to respect rules, I could not help perceiving, perhaps via the aid of darkness and my altered mind, that the rules were only there to provide a pretext. The rules were there to soothe the troubled and take in the gullible. Any realist up to snuff was bound to comprehend that winning existed on a different plane. If you were interested in winning, then, while you needed to make a lot of outward signs indicating rule-respect, internally you needed to admit to yourself that rules, as they say, were created to be broken, and you needed to go about carefully selecting which rules did not pertain to you.

In my infinite wisdom, in the dark, on drugs, I decided, during the course of Murder, that the rule that did not pertain to me was the rule about blindness. In a way, this was a poignant election.

I did not, however, wish to see—at least, not fully. This desire, too, had a deeper significance. Anyway, if I opened my eyes I would also open myself to censure, and after that I would be unable to win.

Therefore, I squinted. It was nearly the middle of the night and all we had was the fire, so things were sort of gummy and smudged. I maintained a posture I felt was accurate to that of a person who was not looking and, for this reason, could not see. I watched as my coworker J.J., whose eyes were wide open (probably another metaphor), pointed across the circle at another coworker, Hailey, even as Gary, in his capacity as Narrator, nodded his acknowledgement.

"It is morning," Gary intoned, after an appropriate interval.

We all opened our eyes. Or, rather, everyone whose eyes had been fully shut opened them.

"There has been a murder. Alas, Hailey was discovered dead!" Gary was doing a pretty good job. He was young and conscientious.

Hailey, who had loudly announced earlier that she had never even heard of this game, appeared perturbed. "Wait, why did I die?" she wanted to know.

"You were undone, dispatched, bumped off," Gary crooned. "You were murdered in the night!"

"But why was *I* murdered?"

Gary started to say something else in character, something about how no one knows the motive of a devious and successful murderer, because the murderer's motive is the first thing that gives a murderer away, but he was interrupted by Nina, our COO, whose phobia of complaints often propelled her into literal explanations. "It's random," Nina said. "It doesn't mean anything."

"I don't get it." Hailey frowned.

"So," Nina continued, "you're quote unquote dead and you're out of the game, so you can just sit there."

"I lost?" Hailey seemed shocked.

"Probably," Nina said.

Gary was still in character. "Death comes when we least expect it. The weeping and the wailing of the villagers could be heard from miles around."

"*For*," I said, which was also in character for me. "It's '*for* miles around.'"

"Thanks!" Gary exclaimed, identifying in me, I could tell, a death wish.

I shrugged.

"So anyways, everyone's really upset and scared and they all go to bed with their doors locked, and once again it was night."

This was the signal for us to shut our eyes. I did the same thing I had done the turn before. I gazed through the furry mesh of my lashes.

I was hoping, perhaps given my pedantic correction of Gary's speech, that J.J. would come for me. But J.J. didn't. She pointed at Nina.

"It's morning and Nina has been garroted," said Gary.

"What!" Nina exclaimed. "We aren't even playing this right. You were supposed to ask if we knew who the murderer was after Hailey died."

Gary was unperturbed. "No one came forward with a theory after that tragic eve. The police were baffled. And now another senseless brutal slaying has rocked the quiet calm of this otherwise unremarkable rural village, somewhat renowned for its high-quality goat cheese and traditional barns."

"Isn't there supposed to be a detective character?" This was J.J. now. "I think I remember playing with a detective."

You had to hand it to her.

"No," said Nina, turning to J.J. "We did it that way last year and it was a problem because the detective always got knocked off immediately. But you *are*," she was addressing Gary now, "supposed to ask for accusations in between every turn."

"I thought I was the narrator."

"Yes. That's what you do. Could you do that, please?"

"I ask for accusations?"

"Yes, please."

Gary sighed. "Are there any accusations?"

No one said anything.

J.J. was like, "Just so I'm clear, the narrator can't be the murderer?"

I kind of wanted to condemn her for overplaying her hand a bit, but then again, I knew a lot more than my fellow villagers and this was a democracy.

Nina smiled. "That's right. The narrator cannot be the murderer." It was funny because here Nina was pitying J.J., and meanwhile Nina did not know yet that J.J. was the one who had rendered her dead.

"Got it." J.J. nodded, apparently taking this in.

"Can I make an accusation?" This was Hailey.

"No," said Nina. "You are dead. You also don't have to close your eyes."

"Oh, so there's a benefit to dying!" Hailey was pleased.

"Are there any accusations?" Gary wanted to know. "It's getting late and it's going to be night soon."

Two people were dead and another person was the murderer and then there was Gary, so that left six of us to run the village with its pungent dairy and well-made barns. I could imagine we were already pretty short-staffed. But I thought about how the murderer was still among us, working enthusiastically alongside us, maybe even more diligent than the rest of us due to psychotic glee, eating our wholesome cheese-based meals and sleeping under our gambrels. In fact, if you counted this demented fiend, there were still seven of us to run the village. So things weren't really all that bad yet, although they were definitely going to get worse.

"Night falls," Gary intoned.

I realized, I don't quite know why or how, that J.J. was not going to execute me. J.J., a talented graphic designer who could always find work even during a recession, was going to pick off other folks first and preserve me for the last. She would come for me near the end, when she could be assured that I would really feel it. For the time being, she was just amusing herself, killing time along with colleagues.

Now she pointed across the circle at Keith.

Gary nodded. He was looking at J.J. *Keith*, he mouthed.

J.J. tipped her head ever so slightly, confirming what Gary was mouthing.

It was a good choice. I felt excited. I wanted to see how

Keith would die. Hailey and Nina had both died really stupid deaths.

"The sun has risen," Gary told us. "Although the villagers gathered together in the night, thinking there was safety in numbers, sadly the goat-herder Keith was not accounted for in the morning. When a search party went out, they found he had been beaten to death with his own shepherd's staff."

Keith was making a face like a corpse that has been beaten to death.

"Oh no!" I whimpered, playing along. "He looks like ground round!"

"Ew," said J.J.

Eugene, who had so far remained silent, raised his hand.

"Yes, Eugene?" said Gary.

"I have an accusation. I feel like Christine [this was me] is very suspicious and I want to accuse her."

"You accuse Christine? Are you sure?"

"Yes. She's trying to get us to believe she's innocent."

"*Excuse me*," I said, turning to Eugene, whom I disliked but usually pretended to tolerate, "how exactly am I trying to get you to think I'm innocent?" I knew this was the very sort of thing that would make me seem guilty, and I really, really wanted Eugene to fuck up.

"No one innocent would say what you just said," Eugene informed me.

"Is that so?" I asked. Eugene clearly did not understand the layers to this game. I looked over at Gary. "Gary, am I the murder?"

"The *murder*?" Gary wanted to know.

"The murderer!" I exclaimed, cheerfully sloshing more liquor into my disposable tumbler.

"Eugene," said Gary, "do you denounce Christine?"

"I do."

"Well, too bad, because she's not the murder or the murderer. You are dead."

"What?"

"She's not the murderer. You're dead."

"But she's acting so guilty!"

"I cannot control Christine," Gary told Eugene, which, in this moment, happened to be true.

And this was, I should say, also the moment when, trembling with my SOLO cup, I saw the way things work, because I saw what this game really was. I had never known it before, the feeling that was currently flowing into my face. I thought of it as the sensation of an encounter with the Truth.

Let's return for a moment to that equation, $g = (D - b)/p$. I had realized, not without a tingle of elation, that by cheating at the game of Murder I'd artificially reduced my blind-spot quantum (b) not to nil but to a value that was so much lower than that of everyone else around me that it might as well have not existed. For isn't everything in this world about context? I had no impediments and as the possible people (*p*) kept dying, my insight (*g*) was grandly growing. It would, for example, have been impossible for me to be so flamboyant with Eugene if I hadn't been assured (1) that he was not the murderer and (2) that his subsequent death would make my inevitable triumph over J.J. all the more sweet.

Also, I could feel Keith looking at me. He picked gently over my face and torso. He had this way of perving out where he appeared to be talking to or appreciating someone else. There was a sort of fuzzy pressure, and when I could feel this, I knew that his eyes were about to snap right onto mine, which was what was going to happen and, then, what did take place.

Keith was thinking, *Fuck this world*. Also he was thinking, *You, Christine, are in this world*. His glassy, sober eyes, black like earth and brown like memory, rolled over mine. He was a wheel and I was terrain, maybe. I was an animal and he was telling me he had some food.

The other thing you need to know about me and my life in this moment, such as it was, is that I had made an attempt earlier that very day to die. Even now I'm not too sure how serious this attempt was but, when you think about it, even having tried is not a thing one should ignore. I was driving, which is the worst and most shameful part of it. I was alone in the car, driving to this retreat, and along the side of a small mountain there was a curve, and I was on the inside lane and another car was coming up the (steep) hill on the outside and I swerved into this car's lane. It was not premeditated. It was not like me. I had only seen a chance.

I swerved back in time and thus was able to continue on within this charming day to make it to the game of Murder. But maybe this was the beginning of my loss of *b*: I was deviating into oncoming traffic. All I knew was that I did not fucking know. And if I didn't know, then why not cheat at Murder?

J.J., meanwhile, kept taking people out. Finally, a morning came when it was just me, J.J., and this guy, Art, a feckless cog with half a PhD, and we all went round and round with Gary, me, and J.J. pretending not to know what the hell was going on and Art doing his usual fumbling. Everyone else had long ago been ready for their beds but still I managed a little scene. "Let's end this charade. I've known," I said, not even lying now, "that it was J.J., all along." And I listed off everything J.J. had said or done for the past twenty minutes, making it sound like a watertight case. My language was rough, my consonants sloppy, but I had that flawless logic that can emerge only from a string of fabrications.

And I convinced them, was the thing. And they believed my genius and looked on me with awe for about ten seconds.

Next, we all got up from the fire, thereby dissolving *D*.

My *g* became abysmal as we stumbled around trying to re-member which rooms of the rented house were assigned to which people.

I was still fresh in this moment, though. Keith, who had stoically volunteered to sleep in the loft of the musty garage out back, a separate and somehow pointy building, hove alongside me, lugging a mattress. "Christine, can I trouble you to help me out?"

I was married, then, you see. And I was very young. And Keith had not been drinking and Keith was not extremely high. The way things work is, everything is possible and ev-erything is permitted. This was what everyone seemed to know, except for me, who was equipped with an extraordi-narily high *b*. This was why my colleagues kept their eyes shut during Murder. And why everyone else, except for me and Keith, just went to sleep.

Keith didn't care about Murder, because Murder was a game. Who knows what he did with his eyes during its "nights." What Keith did care about were limits, and limits were something that Keith did not like.

Here I need, for a moment, to go back in time. I don't think I should go very far, but I'll go a little ways so that you can have a better idea of what sort of narrator I am. If the game of Murder ended around 11:00 p.m., let's do about fourteen hours so we can get a glimpse of me as I appeared earlier that day, circa 9:00 a.m. It is, by the way, a Friday, late July.

I'm sitting on the deck of a modernist construction in the middle of the woods. I'm not yet at my work retreat. Rather, I'm at a much nicer house. It's in Connecticut and it's where my parents live. I'm not, by the way, sitting in a chair. I'm sitting on my butt directly on the wood planks of the deck and my back is against the glass of a floor-to-ceiling window-wall that intervenes between the deck and the interior of the house. Everything about this building is boxes. It's there on a hill on stilts.

I'm sitting in direct sunlight. I have some cold coffee and probably a phone. Ostensibly, I'm here because I'm borrowing my parents' car. I prefer not to be stranded at work-related excursions.

I imagine I'll get tan. Or, I'm soaking up some sort of health. I'm not, to be frank, doing very well. I'm working on my equations.

I think, What is the best way of quantifying another person's face, his handsome grin, his feral stare, those lassoes that shoot out of his eyes . . . ?

Now my mother appears. It's embarrassing because she interrupts my reverie. I'm almost at the point of believing that nothing exists in human social life except for quantities. I've got a very low score these days but hey, at least I have one.

My mother is dressed in one of her Anglo ensembles: she has on a quilted vest and fake jodhpurs.

The sun presses into my face. It sticks its hot, dull fingers in there. It seems to be getting *underneath* my eyes, if this is possible. It slaps me delicately, over and over, everywhere. It looks almost green to me, this light. Dark green, the sun is, striped with black, blotched with violet, a purple-chartreuse-maroon gray. I'm wearing underwear and a T-shirt, although I'm over thirty. Who knows where my father is.

My mother tells me that she's "going into town."

"Right," I say.

We're both looking at my legs, which are long and veal-like. You could still hang me from a hook and sell me as a sort of ingénue. When I was in school we read a lot of British novels, but even accounting for the difference between nineteenth-century and twenty-first-century woman years, I am expiring. This isn't even considering the fact that I am already married, which probably takes the adjustment in my favor of, whatever, like two years away. Nevertheless, my mother would like to sell me once again.

"I could just pick something up for you," she says.

I don't know what this means. In my mind's eye, I see beautiful footwear, flattering dresses, an overpriced T-shirt that changes my life. My mother has never bought this sort of thing for me and has made me pay for all of my own clothing since I was twelve, which is why it comes from the Goodwill even now and why I don't like money. But something in her voice makes me believe that at last something has changed. Is she ready to give me a token of affection, one that comes for free?

Over the past several years, my mother has developed a hobby. If she did not live an almost entirely solitary life with my father she would never be able to get away with having this hobby, but given their nonexistent social circle, which gives rise to a paucity of witnesses, she can. My mother's hobby is not really an activity. It's a character whom she occasionally portrays when she and my father are on vacation. This character's name is Crystal (I'm just guessing at the spelling) and Crystal comes out on cruise ships and at resorts, usually, as far as I can tell, in the evenings, although she can emerge in daylight, too. Crystal likes to volunteer when MCs ask for volunteers. She has a flair for the theatrical and does well with microphones. Crystal hijacks dinner shows and group tennis lessons. People recognize her later and come over to her table. They buy Crystal a drink.

The legend of Crystal has been told to me and my husband, Hank, when we are over at my parents' house for dinner. The legend is introduced by my father, who mutters even when he elects to speak in complete sentences. "Did you know your mother's a star?"

But no one cares what I know or do not know about my mother. It's just a rhetorical question—rhetorical in the sense that it doesn't matter if the audience for the question is/are alive.

Hank will start looking very happy right about now. He'll commence smiling and dangle one arm over the back of his chair. He'll get to work on his eleventh glass of wine.

Hank is an alcoholic but has good skin, small pores. My parents have come to enjoy his company more and more, and their enjoyment seems to occur in direct proportion to the rarity of his presence (it's increasingly rare), as well as the derangement of his senses during the time he shares with them (he's almost always bombed). He is, as far as I can tell, their perfect witness and coconspirator.

"This's gonna be good," says Hank, as if rolling up his sleeves, although he makes no move save to imbibe.

I'm drunk, too, but I don't want to be. Being aware that you do not want to be drunk when you really, really are is not an easy thing to do, but there is a trick that I have learned, to which I made reference earlier when I started going on about my "space of resolve." This trick is to get more drunk. By getting drunker, you become incapable of telling what is going on around you and can at last concentrate on yourself, you, number one. It's a way of having "me time" in company, and what I usually found, once I'd thrown enough fermented liquid down my throat, was that "me" was sad. "Me" wanted to be doing something else. "Me" did not want to be having dinner with these people.

On this night, I was not quite in touch with myself yet. I was still somewhat close to the surface when we started learning about Crystal's latest exploits.

Crystal's story was imparted via dialogue. It wasn't a linear narrative. "You remember when . . . ?" my father asks, mentioning how Crystal cleverly bopped the master of ceremonies over the head with a sourdough baguette when he was getting salty.

"What a surprise," says my father.

My mother giggles.

"Your mother is becoming a superstar. I think we're going to be able to stay for free next season. Your mother was going around to all the tables. They almost called her back on stage. Back by popular demand! He asked her what her name was and she says, 'Crystal.' He says, 'The Mystical Crystal?' She says, 'That depends on who wants to know!' That was just the beginning. Someone said to me, 'You have to take this show on the road.'"

"Roadie," my mother says.

"'Mystical Crystal and Her Roadie,'" says my father.

"I have to keep my public happy," my mother says.

"Your work is never done," says my father.

Hank and I stay at my parents' place overnight. After dinner, we stumble into the downstairs guest room. All I can remember is Hank telling me he wants me to put on these shoes I brought with me in my bag. They're heels with platforms. I have them for a wedding we're actually up here to attend.

I think he ties me to the bed, but I don't remember. He often says things like, "This is what you need," or: "This is what you get."

But where was I? Oh yes, I remember, it's later on in this part of my life, the deck, my mother's offer. She is asking, can she pick something up for me.

"I don't think I need anything," I say, feeling proud. In a moment she'll leave and I can take a shower, and then I'll drive to my trust-building retreat with my office colleagues.

But my mother doesn't leave. She keeps on standing there, overdressed for the summer heat, staring down at me.

"Maybe I can just pick you up a little HPV vaccine?"

It is like a blow.

"What?" I say.

"I just thought, I'm going by the drugstore. Maybe I can just pick you up some vaccine and you can take it."

"You can't *buy* that over the counter," I tell her, as if the problem here is merely that she's misinformed. "You can't *buy* HPV vaccine at the store."

I must seem angry, because my mother giggles and nods. She takes on a hovering quality, her car and house keys clicking against the key fob in her hand. "Will you be here when I get back?"

"Probably not," I say.

And it's true. I won't be. I'm going to be driving a short distance to another state. And near the border between these states I'm going to wind around an ancient, ground-down mountain in the old Volkswagen they're lending me and I'm going to see that determined Chrysler SUV hauling ass up that nearly blind curve, its heavy newness and gleaming grille like a solution, a quantity, I'll see, that fits into all of my equations, because all things, I now know, are equivalent to force. This is the way things work—not through vision but through blindness. And if I swerve toward it, it's because I see. And if I swerve back again, it's because I don't yet know what else I know.

Scary Sites

— So you're asking me if I know, specifically, of another instance of this thing, apart from yours?
— I guess my question is how did you know that? Because I did not.
— I'm trying to think if I know of another instance. In a way it all operates by hearsay, and what you get is an accumulated negative opinion in the next circle out. And of course the opinion does not become uniformly negative. For some people . . .
— They're like, great!
— Like the victor is . . .
— Like, that fucking woman, why did she be a woman?
— Right. Like, why was that cunt a cunt?
— As it's usually put.
— As it's usually put. So, to me, the social effects are—let's

take your example, I do notice every time Cody comes up in conversation and what is said about him. We used to live in a quasi-polite society, so, like, whether those opinions get reflected back into action against this person, however slight, is always unclear.

— He doesn't live here.

— Right, well, like, *before*. But I do know, and I do think this is true, and this is, ha, unfortunately for him, doubly true for people who are in the arts, reputational issues rustle around you in a pretty intense way.

— It's weird because no one seems to know who he is. Like they may have known that I was married for a fair amount of time or something. But they don't know who that person is I was married to. Like, to the extent that, when I moved out of my place, I basically was like, everybody come and take my furniture.

— I remember.

— I was a bit deep in trauma.

— Do you miss any of that stuff?

— No!

— Great.

— It was the best thing I've done in years, and I did it by accident. But someone came over with Phoebe Klein, actually this guy she's married to, I don't even know what his name is. But I had this print by a guy who lives in Iowa, and this guy, Phoebe's husband, was like, are you giving that away? And I was like, oh no. I am not giving the art away! I hope I said that in a nice way. And then this guy was like, oh that's so great, who is it by. And I said, Oren Droste. And he was like, oh, I know him! That's crazy, how do you have his work, he's an esoteric outsider artist. And I was like, yeah, but he teaches at a university.

— He's not really an outsider!

— I mean, what *is* an outsider?

— You know Cody is pretending to be an outsider artist.

— I *know*! Anyway, this guy, Phoebe's husband, was like, how did you get this, and I was like, I used to hang out with these people, and he was like, oh yeah I knew them, or this circle of people, and then it came out that the person he knew best was Cody. And he just said it like that, "Cody Garrison." And I think I had given some generic version of the story in which I said I used to be married to someone who was close to Oren Droste. And after the guy said Cody Garrison, I was like, yes, *that's* the person I used to be married to. And the guy was like, oh. He sort of didn't know what to say.

— Poor schmuck.

— Yeah. And then he said, "Is Cody still in New York?" Because I guess that's the question you ask!

— (laughs) You were like, leave my home.

— I was like, Phoebe, I am sorry that you had a child with this person. Hope it works out.

— (laughing)

— I was like, um, *no*, he doesn't live in New York. I was

like, he—and I mean, I was freaking out internally at this point, I felt like I was in a nightmare—he, Cody, had to leave, I said. I said he did some really bad things. And I just left it at that. And basically Phoebe packed this guy up, her husband or whatever. But it left me in this mode of, this person didn't know where Cody was or anything about his life, and clearly it had been four years since he had spoken to him. And that's the only time that Cody has come up, like with anyone anywhere. And I must have seen, maybe you showed me this, that Roberta Smith tweeted about his work years ago.

— I sent that to you.

— Which made me think, maybe I should do something about this, but then I was like, who cares. It's just another drop in the bucket.

— How would you have responded?

— There's nothing I could say. I mean, I think my main thing has been, actually, I tried to talk to Thomas Rice, be like, Tom, in case, I want to make sure that you know about what happened with this artist. And I've also tried to be like Tom, you should be aware of what happened between me and Darren. I mean, I haven't said that explicitly to him, but I've made it just about as clear as I possibly could without telling him.

— Why does it matter to you that Tom Rice knows that about you and Darren?

— Because Tom has three daughters.

— Wait, they had *another* kid? When did they have another kid?

— Two weeks ago.

— What?

— It's crazy. And they are like, we actually do not know how we are going to pull this out, in terms of real estate and stuff. I was like, how can that be? You guys are both working full time and I assume that your families are wildly wealthy.

— I don't know about him, but she looks very moneyed.

— Well, I think Tom's family is in oil. He's like, super rich. I thought! But what do I know, it's hard to tell what goes on.

— You never know.

— You never know! But I guess it's important to me because Tom is somebody who entered a certain space and like his relationship was criticized by his friends as being uxorious. There was some—OK, this is weird gossip—but there was some intervention.

— Before they married?

— Yeah.

— You know that she is supposedly on Tinder? Have you heard this?

— What?

— Oh yeah.

— That sounds like a crazy rumor!

— To be clear, the rumor comes from Danny French, who is a congenital and compulsive liar.

— That's really mean! And I think that may be a symptom of—I think a lot of these guys who are in that circle are really intimidated by this woman.

— Why do you think that?

— Because she's very successful, professionally, and she doesn't really, there's like no empathy coming from her at all. And in a certain way she's hard to pity. Like I think people pity Alana, for example. They're like, oh she's such a genius, but she's so emotionally fucked up. I don't know. I need to get away from all this stuff. I find it so emotionally toxic.

— (laughing)

— (laughing)

— Have you had this conversation with people?

— It's just, every conversation is that! That's the message about Alana. And I'm just like, I do not know this person!

— Do you not? Have you never spent time with her?

— I mean, I have. But I don't know her! Anyway, this is all neither here nor there, and I am saying mean things. But I think it's interesting, because Tom is in this kind of double position, where he's made these alliances with different white men, and French, for example, has talked to me about how he specifically seeks out other straight white men to work with because it's a good way to make money.

— That's the most French thing ever.

— It was amazing to hear someone say that.

— Talk about pulling the veil back!

— It was interesting to see someone take that route. But with Tom, there are other routes where he's like, I'm all about, like, diversity! But, then, he has this situation where he lives with four women. And he has three daughters. And I think for him, this is just a theory, but he's like, oh fuck I see how my friends have treated women, what they've said about them, what they've explicitly told me they would do and then did.

— Wait. Other than French, who are you talking about?

— I don't know but, like, I told you that stuff Darren said to me about how he and Alejandro would behave at parties.

— As in?

— They would have these plans for women, like for picking women up, that they would then execute.

— But that doesn't seem hyper-misogynistic to me. That just seems like a thing that straight guys have done since time immemorial.

— Oh, it seems hyper-misogynistic to me, but that is probably because I'm super naïve.

— You can do that in a hyper-manipulative way then having succeeded treat the woman badly, or you can ingratiate yourself according to basic laws of human behavior, like the kinds of things they teach you in the FBI, like here's how to make someone trust you, it's just steps 1 2 3 4 5. So you can use those for bad ends or good. It could be used against either sex.

— It's not specific, except insofar as they were not targeting other men.

— Sure. They were doing it for a specific end.

— (laughing)

— (laughing) I'm not necessarily defending this sort of behavior.

— I mean, men can jerk each other off, too.

— I don't find this shocking.

— All I'm saying is, I've had this theory about Tom for a long time.

— So many theories about such a boring person!

— He's not boring!

— He's boring.

— He's really funny! He is. I think he's a very good public speaker.

— (laughing) Because that's all that matters. That is damning with faint praise, if I have ever heard it.

— I'm horrible.

— How are you doing?

— I'm OK. I guess I look at other people's behavior and I'm like, do they think I'm a marked human? One of the last things Cody said to me—this was over the phone before I hung up on him—was, "You're always going to be a victim." And the implication was, this is why this happened, because you *are* a victim.

— What he was implying, I think, was, not because you *are* a victim but because you conceive yourself to be one.

— Yes. But the point was, you inspire these kinds of actions in other people. To me, when I heard him say that, I felt there was a kind of aggression, whether it was conscious or not. That, while he might have thought he was saying, this is a performance that you do because you can't stand to occupy any other kind of role, I think he was also saying, like, that's actually your role, is to be a victim for people who need to do some fucked-up thing.

— It's possible that's what he meant.

— I don't think he heard himself saying that. That's just the way it sounded to me.

— Was this in the context of a fight?

— This is in the context of him saying, I don't know why— we were talking on the phone—maybe he wanted to pick some stuff up at the house, I don't remember. I mean, it was just really hard to go from being with someone for eleven years to not speaking to them. I may have even initiated the conversation. I think what happened was I was like, hey, you lied to me for a really long time. Why did you do that? That was really fucked up.

— And what did he say?

— That was when he said it. Well, the first thing he said was you never loved me, and the second was, you're a victim and you'll always be a victim.

— So, to further extrapolate, what he was saying was, it's your fault, you forced me to behave this way.

— Exactly. And that is what I wanted to ask you about, the invisible social effects. I think that Darren took a similar position, he was like, you're crazy, you're out of control, no one who wants to have the kind of professional success I want to have could be your partner because you're so crazy.

— You're not a good gala wife.

— Exactly.

— And I was like, but I'm pretty!

— Oh no.

— And he was like, your ass is too sexy. And I was like, this is not going to end well.

— What I was talking about is more a kind of quiet reputational harm that can happen—which *is* the case with Cody but less with Darren, because you had a preexisting and highly public social contract with Cody.

— I still have that contract, even.

— I bet you do. So, the invisible social effects are liable to be greater with Cody because anyone who is in the little ripple around you two has some version or other of what happened and to the extent there's a whisper network, or shunning, or changes in opinion that may never ever even become explicit but will in some way affect how that person is treated for a long time, like, I can't give you empirical evidence about how it operates, but I know that it does, because I do it, and other people do it, too, so we know it's real.

— I think with both of them I was freaked out because their take on this was, you're crazy and you're projecting and that's why all of this happened, essentially. Because you didn't have a good grip on reality.

— What does that have to do with the situation with Cody?

— I think he was saying that I thought that I was being a partner in a normal way, but actually what I was doing was really fucked up and no one could live with me. That was the thing that he said to me, no one could live with you. Which is what is so hard for me to understand, because for years I'd been picking him up off the floor and carrying him back to the house. And I was kind of like, no one could live with me?! Like, I thought the whole thing about our relationship was that I took care of you? And that was really—I'm still shocked by that. It's so hurtful to me. I was giving up a lot of stuff to be with him. It was stupid of me, which is why it's great that the relationship ended, but it did a lot of damage. But the same thing was true of Darren, because I would listen to him all the time when he would talk about his insecurities and I would just be like, no, you're great! Like, don't worry about it, you've got this. He used to call me all the time when he would have a bad meeting with somebody, and I would say, don't listen to that asshole, you're a good person and things will work out.

— He was like, they didn't give me enough money!
— No, that's what would happen! I was so naïve! I was such a naïve fool. And then, later, he sort of said the same thing, like, you're too unstable or something, and I was like, but my marriage of eleven years just ended and you'd be unstable, too. But that's the thing I started to be really afraid of—that everyone I knew also saw me that way. Like, as being someone who just projects things, who is really out of control, and I was worried because I didn't feel like I was behaving this way, I felt like I was trying to support both of these people. So it's those effects that I'm trying to understand. And it sounds like it's mostly within me and has nothing to do with the objective world, so called.
— Right, right. I mean, I can really only speak for myself.
— OK.
— I mean, because I don't know how others saw you during that period, because they didn't tell me.
— That's good. (laughing)
— (laughing) So I don't have a lot of empirical information on that front. I guess I would say doesn't everybody expect someone going through a divorce to be highly unstable? Isn't that even what society wants from you?
— I think so.
— Aren't you just fulfilling a role in a way?
— OK, so, there are roles, and then there are these social effects that are associated with gossip.

— Yeah.

— But I felt like when we talked about this before you were also talking about something that comes from the person themselves, the aggressor?

— I completely think that's true.

— So, what is that?

— The truth is that I don't know that many of those aggressors ever deal with it, but it's inside. Like, I can guarantee you that if either of those two people ever took a solid dose of psychedelics they would be dwelling on their situation with you for a good portion of time. It's the kind of thing that gets trapped in there and like maybe you deal with it ten years later or twenty, but whenever you strip off the first layer of mind—I can say from experience that you don't give up the times that you've hurt people. They come up really fast and strong when your mind is able to see it. It's all in there.

— It's like the ghosts of genocided aliens? Like in Scientology?

— There's a "th" word for it?

— I don't know.

— It is a "Thetan"?

— Yes! They're Thetans! That's really good that you know that.

— I was like, "Thanatos"? But it's not Thanatos. (laughing)

— (laughing)

— No, but those things are—I can only speak analogically

because I have not perpetrated anything like this, but when my conscious mind is not in control, I mean, a drug is just one example. It could be dreams, it could be grief, or whenever you find yourself in an unusually vulnerable situation, that stuff is very close to the surface. The body does not forget about those things.

— This is really helpful because when my mind is not in control or doing whatever it does to produce consciousness, for me everything goes back to something that happened to me when I was a child that I don't understand at all and it's really horrible. I don't know what it is, I can't see it; it's so scary that I can't see it, or look at it, and it's like everything that has happened to me interpersonally since then doesn't even show up. It makes it really difficult for me to understand how it is for people who are picking up these things as they go. I think in a way there's some truth in what Cody was saying about me always being a victim.

— Interesting.

— I have a kind of aphasia. I can't understand how people change as adults. I'm stuck.

— This is probably difficult to answer and why would you know, but, are you sure that there is an event associated with this thing, or is it possible that it is just a miasmic malevolence that has filtered into your way of being and has no specific and singular cause?

— I thought for a while that it was that, that it was a series of things that tipped something and became something that the sensorium couldn't process anymore (coughing). Sorry (coughing). Sorry, when I start talking about it I get physical symptoms. It's always associated with my throat. That's all I know. The other weird thing is I know that both Cody and Darren were people whose parents beat them up. I think Cody had it bad in a lot of ways, particularly because he had a lot of allergies and circulatory and respiratory things that were caused by his mother smoking when she was pregnant, and for years they had a dog that he had terrible allergies to, and he couldn't breathe. This is a thing that causes me to have a really deep connection to people, but it's a connection that's along something that's so fucked up, I really don't want to keep doing it.

— So are you saying, common victimhood? Is that what it is?

— Maybe. Or maybe it's a thing where there's something that happened, but the person doesn't have access to it. Like Cody would never talk about this stuff. I just know it through bits and pieces. Darren was aware of what had happened to him, and all of his mania about making money and having success is basically about avoiding being the person someone's hitting. Which is why I empathized with him so excessively.

— Too bad it made him unbearable.

— Yeah.

— He is not well liked, I hope you know.

— I've gotten that impression.

— In part from envy, but just, in general. He's in that world and people are like, fuck that guy.

— I think he represents a lot of stuff that hurts other people. He took one path in relation to harm. Anyway, what you're saying about the internal things is helpful. It makes sense. But then the question is, how does that play out for that person? I don't know whether it's in terms of their feelings or their actions or how they live. Are they always running away from that?

— I don't know. I know very little about theories of mind. I've never studied them, aside from a stray Freud essay here or there.

— But what's your intuition?

— My intuition is that disordered behavior results from these things, and the way that disordered behavior manifests happens differently depending on the person, but I think it gives rise to impulses or desires or compensations that remain mostly invisible. We build up fortresses of ideas. And it does affect a person to have a fortress in their brain.

— So, how should society react? Let's just pretend it's the nineteenth century and we can have these kinds of conversations! Because we're going back there anyway, you know.

— But this is the central disorder of human existence.

— It's what tragedy is based on, you mean?

— This is the disorder of our world. This is why we have everything.

— We're completely on the same page.

— This is our sickness. That's what it is. (laughing)

— (laughing) Right, but so, how should we react to it? I'm not denying its centrality.

— (laughing) This is why everyone in 1967 felt like it would be good to take LSD and meditate and make the Pentagon lift off the ground.

— Is that what we should do now?

— I sometimes think about this in relation to the way people use social media. On the one hand, everyone has to use social media in a somewhat performative way. And they have to come to terms with the voice they use. For some people it's a very false voice, like a picture, like "This is who I am!"

— Shrill.

— Or, "This is what I'm dealing with." There is a counter-current to performativity where people are like, this incredibly intense thing has happened and I'm telling a lot of people. I'm having horrible issues in my marriage or someone close to me died in a really horrible way, or my kid is incredibly sick or I'm really sick or I'm infertile.

— I was fired.

— Right. I was fired, or I'm going to call out my harasser; things it was impossible to be honest about in the past. Or you could potentially use the press.

— As long as you weren't harassed by Harvey Weinstein.

— Right.

— In which case you could not use the press.

— So, in our society I feel there's a lot of duplicity, but there is also a countercurrent of candor. Which is interesting. I'm not saying that the candor itself is not in some way performative. It often is.

— Or self-exploitative?

— It's a very mixed bag. But one thing I will say is that certain stigmas are being shattered and in service of what is always a question. I'm not going to deny that aspect of it. I'm merely identifying a current. People are different about this stuff than they were a half century ago or even a quarter. It's one of the few things in our society that I think is OK.

— Yesterday I was taking this bus, and it had these movie screens in it? And for some reason they played the Steve Jobs movie with Ashton Kutcher.

— Did you watch it?

— I didn't listen to the sound but I would gaze up. There's something very revealing about watching a movie without sound. You find out what it's about. And it's amazing because the movie is about, I mean, there are like two female characters in it; it's just all about these mostly white men and how they get together in these windowless rooms and they're like, we have this idea that only we can understand, let's use it to make money. That's what the movie's about. And then, at the end, suddenly Steve Jobs is in a garden with his wife, who's put him in touch with the earth, and he's reunited with Lisa Brennan-Jobs, who's sleeping on the couch, and he has a loving non-incestuous relationship with her, although he steals her blanket. And then he goes and dies, but we don't see that. I mean, Ashton Kutcher is a moron and he's playing a genius, and it kind of works in this interesting way if you don't listen to the sound. It's like an L.L.Bean catalogue.

— Ashton's very L.L.Bean.

— I love his emotions. He's like a muppet. But I did think about how it's the last time we can tell this story in this way. Like there'll be a niche show where there's a Midwestern guy with a beer belly and a beer and it's like, oh you're so crazy, and he's like, I'm so crazy, but there won't be this Knights-of-the-Round-Table sort of thing. I'm just saying I see this occurring on a representational plane. I don't know what it means for actual people.

— Yeah.

— I do know that in classes I teach I consistently have a white guy who writes super-violent, exploitative stuff. That guy's always there.

— Do you call that person out?

— There are some things I can say, but they are dissociating and it can be dangerous. The people I've dealt with so far are genuinely ill. I have a really bad one right now. It's this guy who's written a story that takes place in "Hispaniola" and it's about this girl who's raped in incredible detail. And it's like eighty pages long and he's completely done with it and has handed it in and is like, respond to this now! It's written in a magical realist style. It could not be more awful.

— Oh.

— This is a trend.

— I feel bad for white men, and bear with me, because I think they do this to say, I'm relevant.

— But they can be raped and beat up, too!

— No, I know. But they're like, I'll never get anywhere because I'm not trans or a person of color. This is a thing that white men feel. Hard core. So they're like, oh, I should make art about those things. I'm not kidding. Like this person doesn't see that they're being appropriative. They just think they're engaging with the issues of their time.

— It's scary.

— I know.

— It's unreadable, these descriptions of penetration. I'm like, we don't need—we get how this works, mechanically.

— I would put money on the fact that he believes that he's woke and engaged.

— I think the part of him that's conscious is also thinking, I really enjoy these scenes. I'd like to see more violence like this.

— Did you read *Preparation for the Next Life*?

— No, but I have it. Mike gave it to me.

— If you ever read it, I want to know. It has the most violent and disgusting rape scene I've ever read in any piece of literature. I just felt it was exploitative. I don't know if that's defensible on my part.

— Mike has a lot of interest in violence.

— The other night I was trying to explain why I thought it was not a good book because of this rape scene. I mean, it is a good book. But it's melodramatic. The book is sodden with sentimentality and melodrama. And the linchpin of the sodden-ness is this revolting rape scene.

— That's very nineteenth century.

— Indeed. So I was trying to explain to people how I was impressed by the book but I morally object to it.

— It's like *The Road*.

— Tell me, doctor, how can I defend my opinion using the proper tools?

— I think you already did.

— If rape is just a fictional tool, why is it objectively objectionable to use that tool?

— I think that trying to argue that something that happens in a book is objective is usually a mistake.

— That's not what I'm saying.

— But I think that's part of the difficulty you're having. You don't have to decide that other people have to accept your argument. I think you can say that you think that this rape scene is designed to elicit a kind of prurient interest.

— This is what I said.

— In violence.

— It is.

— Do a comparison. For example, the most violent thing I've ever read is in this Joyce Carol Oates novel called *Zombie*, which is about a psychopath slash serial killer slash rapist who has a fantasy about creating a passive sex slave who will love him forever, and he reads something or sees something somewhere about lobotomies and tries to give lobotomies to—

— His victims.

— His victims. It's so disturbing. And what's so disturbing is not the act of trepanation or whatever you want to call it, putting holes in someone's head or putting a stick in there. It's the period of time when he tries to keep the zombie alive.

— Right.

— I feel like I'm going to vomit. It isn't about someone being beaten in the present, it's about the way in which things that have already happened are leading to events in the present. Leading to hopes that inspire violence, that inspire enslavement, even in the face of death, even in the face of the fact that the victim is already dead and this completely passive object and you can't *do anything more* to control them. So, if I were going to try to criticize the Lish book I would set up a comparison between the two and talk about why what Joyce Carol Oates shows you in this super-exploitative book—because who's more exploitative than she is?

— Number one. Number-one exploiter.

— I would be like, look how much more disturbing this is. And look at what you're being disturbed by. And look how agency is being deployed in the Lish book and don't be fooled. And once you say that, the reader is like—

— I surely would not want to be fooled.

— My strategy.

— I suppose I don't have to read this Oates book.

— Don't read it! I remember when I was sixteen or seventeen, I guess I was trying to read all her novels and I came to this one and read it all in one night and had this horrible cold clammy sweat and was like, why?!! Why?!?

— God. A mere high-schooler.

— That was when I was really at my best.

— Reading-wise?

— Reading-wise and also just—no, I mean, I like myself better now, but that was the time when I look back on how I behaved and I'm always like, that was the way!

— Acting out on the reg.

— Do you need to go back to your desk?

— Not yet. What have we not gotten to?

— The reason I was up all night. It's that I was trying to write this talk for Friday I've been meaning to write all week but just been too scattered. I've been thinking a lot about satire, and this talk is about satire and realism and the ways I see them being interrelated. And about how people have a misapprehension of what satire is, how they think it's like an insult or a hyperbolic portrayal but it's actually a more complex, older category.

— This week's flap about the correspondents' dinner is a perfect example of the misapplication of satire.

— Exactly. It's interesting to me that the thing that was so upsetting to people was actually the one satirical moment. That thing about the perfect smoky eye.

— That was the one true satire?

— Everything else was basically insults. Cheap shots. And if you look at the recent jokes, like Hasan Minhaj's jokes or the lady from SNL whose name I can't remember who I find very generic, they all told exactly the same jokes. That's what I find really strange! Everyone's like, this is all so original, but it's all exactly the same.

— I didn't watch Hasan or the person before that.

— Hasan is very beautiful.

— Isn't he?

— You're just like, oh say anything.

— Just say it out of your beautiful mouth.

— But anyway it's all exactly the same jokes. You know there was a media blackout around Colbert's thing?

— I vaguely remember that.

— It was an emergency in 2006 in a way that this thing in 2018, it's really just a topic that's being offered up. Like, oh yeah, she's a brassy lady who doesn't wax her pussy, etcetera, so let's say mean things.

— But wait, how does this relate to the question of satire?

— Well, it used to be that novels and other forms of literature partly existed to explain these things to us, to explain invisible things, to be like—

— Here's human interiority; now you can understand what's happening.

— Right. Edith Wharton's like, here's a guy who doesn't consummate a relationship; or, Henry James is like, here's a guy who doesn't consummate a relationship; or, Virginia Woolf is like, here's a guy, who doesn't consummate a relationship. And they're like, here's why! It's a very common theme. And it seems like we are in this moment when—I'm having trouble describing it except by calling it the intersection of satire and realism.

— Hmm.

— Realism is just a mode of novel-making that talks about the event as secular. Realism emerges when you have secular events that are produced by the confluence of material conditions and human history. And there's no god. But satire is an older category. It's an older democratic category predating Christianity. It comes from Latin: it's a medley; literally, it's a full plate. It has nothing to do with s-sa-say—how do you say that word?

— Satyrs? I always heard about satyrs.

— It sounds too much like the Passover dinner! So I'm trying to think about that in relation to laughter but also in relation to the idea that literature can be a place where information is leaked.

— Right.

— Literature used to exist to share information that couldn't be shared otherwise. And it seems like social media does not obviate that. And the correspondents' dinner joke is another site where you can have that information leak. That's why I thought that Michelle Wolf's observation about Sarah Huckabee Sanders's smoky eye is true satire. It's very intricate. Like, there is this concept, The Perfect Smoky Eye™ that exists, and, like, if you're not female, chances are you don't know what that is. Like, I don't mean you don't know what it refers to; you don't know what its deeper meaning is, what meaning is encoded in it. It has to do with female aggression and control of the visual realm, and it also has to do with how women have entered the white-collar workforce. There's a lot of stuff in that term that she was pointing to by using it. Which is actually, I think, a lot scarier and more unstable than other things she said.

— So, people had misinterpreted the comment but correctly identified the scary site within it?

— I think it doesn't happen by accident. It stands out because there is something there. There's a form of privacy being invoked.
— What's the form of privacy?
— A series of codes.
— That aren't made public, typically?
— Yeah.
— Interesting.
— I think that's what's threatening to people, that they are like, oh I am not up to date. And it happened in a very condensed way. It's even hard to understand the metaphor as a joke. Like, she burns lies, I mean, she burns *facts*, and then uses the ash, from the facts, for her makeup. Is that a joke? That seems like a weird metaphor you would read in someone's short story.
— It's kind of ornate.
— She was working really hard to sell it. She ended up being like, hey, it's a tough room, but it wasn't really a good joke.
— I thought it was a very good joke.
— I mean, I liked the phrase, "The Perfect Smoky Eye," but the setup didn't work for me.
— It has metaphorical integrity. She's saying that she uses lies as a public face. There's no missing link in the metaphor. It wasn't sloppy.
— It was too literal. But I did like it as being associated with some form of Christianity. Like she's burning them in

her brazier. And I was like, oh I remember this from the Bush II presidency!

— You're like, very evocative. Rich allusions here.

— That would have been my comment. If I had seen that on a student paper. I would have been like, very good! Vehicle needs work!

The Care Bears Find and Kill God

Whenever I was on a plane, I used to listen to a certain helpful voice. The words it spoke came from a meditation script I had found in a PDF online by googling "meditation script fear flying," and the audio file I was listening to was in fact a recording of my own voice as I read the script aloud, huskily and I hoped persuasively, into my phone late one night in the old apartment where I don't live anymore.

Thus, this voice was me.

I still have the file, by the way. The recording was approximately twenty minutes long and before each flight I'd calculate how many times I'd need to play it before landing. Today was six. I gripped the slender armrests of my aluminum beach chair, rented at significant cost, approximately \$3.30 per minute, or 5.5 cents per second. I searched the weary faces of passing flight attendants. Meanwhile, my own voice, reedy but distinct, was piped through noise-canceling headphones, impressing upon me a series of visions: a cabin near a river sheltered by birches; sunlight on cool grass; water reflecting mottled brightness onto the bottom of a rowboat freshly painted a friendly, jaunty, fresh, very fresh and jaunty, friendly, bright brick red.

This soothing projective landscape appeared and disappeared, pinged in and out.

"I would like," my recorded self told myself, "to talk to you about your panic attacks while flying."

As my recorded self uttered the word "while," a distant police siren became audible. This siren came from the past.

I, the listener on the airplane, nodded.

I was saying in the recording, "You are going to be OK. Worrying is not going to make you feel any safer. In fact, worrying will serve no purpose except to exacerbate your panic attack. Worrying leads to panic attacks when flying."

This was the beginning. This meant that there was still a long ways to go. The former version of myself who spoke seemed to believe in her script. She was deeply, or at least presently, convinced. When she said the word "safe" she really sold it, like the *s* and the *f* were made of some sort of sustainable polar fleece, as if there truly was a form of comfort that could be derived, fabricated, even as one was levitating here at high velocity inside a metal tube.

The recording said, "The thing you can control the most right now is your own thinking. When people feel anxious or experience panic attacks when flying, they often have upsetting images go through their minds. If you are feeling anxious right now or have panic attacks when flying, you probably have scary thoughts. It is OK to acknowledge those thoughts and images. Let's do that now."

Yes, I thought, let's. Let's go ahead and do that now and forever. I am feeling anxious. Let's try a thing.

But not much took place. My brain was jellied mush. Nothing was known and nothing remembered. It was really not very good to be this far up in the air, and I was bad at it.

In the recording, I was still going on about mental peace. "Thoughts that lead to panic attacks when flying include thoughts like these: Maybe the plane will crash. Or perhaps you think you aren't getting enough air or that there is a hole in the plane. Maybe you think other people are thinking negative things about you. Maybe you think the plane is going to blow up. Maybe you think someone is going to hijack the plane. Maybe you think the pilot might fall asleep. Maybe you think the wings of the plane will come loose and fall off. Maybe you think the plane will fall out of the air. Maybe you think the plane will catch on fire. Maybe you think the plane will catch on fire and crash as it, smoking and crashing and falling and burning, burns."

Nice use of faux-naïve hyperbole, I thought to myself, as I always did when I came to this sentence, which was partly improvised. I also thought: Dear recording of my former self, you know this is not what I am thinking, that this is not what I fear. I don't care what the other people on this plane think about me, and what I fear has nothing to do with anything that has ever before transpired in the history of human aviation. What I fear is terrifying because it cannot happen and yet it must: this plane will fall upward. It must fall up, out of the Earth's gravitational field, and it must fall up and out and away and into the vast lightless oceans of space in which there is no up nor down nor west nor south, etc. We'll bathe in entropy.

I visualized stripy colorless surrounds, wobbling with narrative instability—my body's collision with the infinite.

Nothing in the meditation script discussed this problem. But, as I had tuned out in favor of said deadly-errors-in-deep-space fantasy, the script was getting pretty far along. Now I was saying, "A small path leads from the cabin door to a dock. A rowboat floats next to the dock."

I marveled, for the millionth time, at these words. I marveled at the familiarity of "rowboat." I marveled at the familiarity of water against painted wood (and such an attractive, classic red).

We were almost done here. My voice began to soar.

"Panic attacks cannot hurt you! You are free from panic attacks when flying! Free because you know that even if you experience panic, you will get through it. The panic will go away. It will not last long. It is no big deal! Since you know that anxiety is no big deal, you have no fear of becoming anxious! You are not even worried about your former fears because you know that you can do it! You are getting through this, right now! You're here right now and you're OK, even if you feel anxious, even if you feel afraid, you're here. You're coping. You're getting through this experience, and you are going to be just fine. You will get through it and feel so good and be so proud of yourself when this is over, because you can look back and know that you got through this. You are doing well! You are able to fly without panic attacks, experiencing no more panic attacks when flying, no more panic attacks when flying or in airports or when thinking about flying or seeing images of airplanes or dreaming about the future of the human race! Just calm! Feeling confident! No more panic attacks when flying! No more panic attacks when flying! No more panic attacks when flying! No more panic attacks when flying. Finished with panic attacks when flying. Overcoming panic attacks when flying. You can go to the airport and board a plane and fly and feel calm throughout the process. You can get through it with ease. You are so much stronger than the panic you have experienced in the past.

"Goodbye," my voice said.

The recording ended.

I listened to it five more times.

Then, much as I could have foreseen had I been thinking clearly, the plane returned to earth without incident, and I was in Chicago.

Now, Chicago is not my favorite American city, but I was here for work. It was the middle of a warmish winter, a gusty season. I got in a cab to my hotel.

I had slept for approximately three hours the night before and yet was obliged to head straight to a meeting. When you work for very rich people, you are always moving around on their time. The people I was working for were very, very much pertaining to that category. No time in these moments belonged to me.

I mean, I worked for one of their subordinates, an unpleasant Canadian named Tim. I'm not sure, by the way, that Tim was, in or of himself, unpleasant. He was an art dealer, and he seemed to like to mess with me, so I suppose that makes him unpleasant, but I also liked to imagine that there were people to whom Tim was not unpleasant, whom he treated with respect and who smiled and felt genuine warmth at the sight of him.

From time to time, Tim sent me emails with subject lines like, "Because I know this will bother you." The body of the email would contain either no text or something brief to the effect that he had made a discovery at an auction or through another dealer. In either case, body text or no body text, Tim attached an image. Always, it was pornographic. Usually, it was vintage.

I am female and was fairly sure that Tim was gay, but he was correct that these missives bothered me. They bothered me because I am (human and therefore) sensitive to images. I am particularly sensitive to images of naked women, about which I have many different kinds of feelings, foremost among which are (*A*), fear that, by means of this image, someone or multiple people are being exploited, and (*B*), intense titillation. I love images of women and I love women, although I mostly sleep with men.

Tim had read a lot of my writing as a function of the work we did together, and perhaps he knew this about me. Perhaps he understood that by sending me a set of collages by a male adherent of an obscure Czech surrealist collective active during the interwar period that included a spotty clipping from an example of late nineteenth-century girl-on-girl (and I do mean "girl," as in pubescent) porn, he was pressing on an aspect of my life that was unstable and which I preferred, therefore, whenever possible, to ignore. But I have to imagine that much of what Tim did when he sent me these messages was automatic if not unconscious; I don't think he meant to hurt me.

Tim worked in an unregulated market and mostly did

what he pleased. I was his contractor: not quite an underling but not an equal, either. I wrote copy for his objects. He paid me. The objects sold. I was the softness that lent things glamour and made them popular. I drew a magic circle.

Tim had flown me out to the Windy City because he needed me, as ever, to look at stuff. This was why my body was present. We were convening in the apartment of an important collector. Tim required a description of a rare and major antique book now in the possession of this major collector. He needed detail regarding prints in the book, which were the creations of the most famous artist known to Western art. He desired me to behold the volume in person, to channel its textures and pigments, scent and heft; I must reproduce its aura. I was the one who could ensure that at last the collector "got it." These were always his words: so-and-so *gets* it. We're having so much fun. We're collaborating on [insert euphemism for exorbitant shopping]. Such is, by the way, the destiny of culture.

My eyes were two lints in my skull and I wanted to sleep, but I couldn't and didn't. I took a hot shower. I walked a few blocks from my hotel to a high-rise where the collector and the intimates of the collector stayed. It was a forty-plus-floor elevator ride, and the wood-paneled box clicked and trembled the whole way up. I felt a combination of uncertainty and awe and wished to be, instead, standing knee high in dirt, down below rather than way up here, melting upward into air.

When I was released, I stepped into a long hall painted

matte black, at the end of which there was a door, gilded in outline. A voice said, "She is here!"

The door was opened by a slender woman in a lemon caftan and pressed pants. Her hair was gunmetal. Her face was smooth, although not youthful; her eyes could not really be reached. This was the collector.

"Here she is." This was Tim, who stood behind the collector in an empty white foyer. When I seemed not to know what to do, he said, "Come in."

Tim and the collector must have been embroiled in some pretty deep talk about valuable whatever. It was less that I had interrupted them than that they regretted their decision to invite me, although they knew they needed meaning and that was something I apparently had and could provide. Now they just needed to get me not to look at the two of them too closely, while also getting me to look at this renowned book and its prints a whole lot.

Tim had warned me that the collector was unusual. He had mostly told me nothing else about anything that was going to happen today, except for the matter of the book. All he would say over the phone was that he thought I "would really enjoy this." He kept repeating that I was going to "flip." He was vague but sort of threatening. "You're not going to be able to get over this one!"

I knew this was in part to psych me up for my performance. It did not matter that I would have gladly lain down on the floor and slept for a day in this priceless hallway. I needed to appreciate anything and everything I saw in the place. It was of the essence that I keep speaking about anything I might see. They weren't paying me not to provide constant verbal flow.

"What a beautiful apartment!" I exclaimed. I was just looking at a bunch of white walls for the moment, but I had to start somewhere.

My voice was creaky, due to diverse altitudes plus lousy climate. I was offered a glass of water, which I gratefully accepted. The collector went away and got it. We were apparently alone with her, no staff.

"Well," said Tim, "you're sort of on time. How was your flight?" He was wearing a turtleneck and, somewhat less successfully, a gray suede vest. He was neat, but not unflappable. He looked like he wished that he could take my face somewhere and wash it.

Before I had a chance to answer, the collector reappeared in a subtle cloud of sandalwood. She handed me a tooth glass. "It's not vodka."

Her face was impassive.

I drank.

"Come on," said Tim, suddenly impatient. He removed the tooth glass from my hand.

"Oh, how fun," said the collector. "Go ahead and hang a left."

She was pointing where she wanted me to go.

It was a small room, beautifully finished: walls of cream

and recessed lighting. At the center of this room was something very, very weird.

Before I go on, I just want to mention: There is no need to
become anxious. Everything turned out OK, or mostly. Later
on I even got to see the rest of the collector's apartment,
which was so high up that one could see the curvature of the
planet. It was, to be sure, an unusual point of view.

The way the place had been designed, when you walked
in, as I've noted, you were in low-ceilinged spaces, traditional
rooms, so you might have thought that this was the situation
throughout—but you would have been wrong in thinking
this, if you had. You only had to pass beyond this warren: the
living room encompassed several stories, somewhat more
than two. Its sill-less windows, meeting the edge of the living
room's floor, made me want to vomit. Grayly, infrastructure
squirmed below.

At least there was art up here, I thought, and therefore I
could look at it. I turned away from the impressive view. The
collector, whom I had misjudged and who was even slightly
shy, was making gentle comments. She ushered us into a side
gallery, chatting. We were done with our work, and she felt
casual.

Now we stood before a famous painting from a ca-
lamitous year, 1939's *El suicidio de Dorothy Hale*, a.k.a.
The Suicide of Dorothy Hale, by Frida Kahlo, an incredible

possession, to say the least. It is so beautiful, this artwork, that it is nearly impossible to describe. It is, first of all, a failed commission. Executed in the style of devotional painting or *retablo*, it partakes of a mystical delicacy to portray a violent death. In the background: a staggered deco apartment building looms in mist. There is a sense of feathers or lace, and the surreal weather has been extended out onto the very frame of the painting. Kahlo selectively stops time, showing what appear to be four moments in Hale's demise within a single, everlasting present. A figure at once appears in a tall window, jumps, tumbles wrapped in mist, lies dead in the foreground: simultaneous narration. Blood soaks the earth below her and forms a web on her cheek, emerging from her ear. In the two instances in which we see Hale's face, her small dark eyes stare, unblinking. "This is how it happens," she may say. Defunct upon the ground, she wears a black evening gown, yellow bouquet pinned near the shoulder.

Kahlo was paid $400 for this ex-voto, which bears a legend at its base, written in red slashes, as if with the corpse's blood: *En la ciudad de Nueva York el día 21 del mes de octubre de 1938, a las seis de la mañana, se suicidó la señora Dorothy Hale tirándose desde una ventana muy alta del edificio Hampshire House: En su recuerdo* [words painted out] *este retablo, habiéndolo ejecutado FRIDA KAHLO.* The missing words are "Clare Boothe Luce," an editor, writer, and friend of the deceased socialite, "commissioned." Boothe Luce,

114

upon receiving what she saw as a gory stunt instead of the respectful portrait she believed herself to have purchased as a gift for the dead woman's mother, had her name painted out by Hale's former lover, the sculptor Isamu Noguchi[1], and dispensed with the work, which was lost in obscure storage until the 1960s.

I was surprised to see this picture here: I was pretty sure that it belonged to a regional museum. I also thought that the edifice we were currently standing in looked a little too much like the edifice depicted for comfort (never mind this was a different city), which gave the whole painting the quality of a cry for help, although whose cry it was I wasn't sure.

"Oh my god," I said, because most of what I was thinking I was not supposed to say.

"You called?" asked Tim.

I didn't say anything after this. I allowed myself to be led around.

Some of the furniture in this place could be obtained from Design Within Reach. Some of it could not.

Tim had been inside this apartment many times before, a fact to which he made frequent reference. I was not so fatigued that within my extreme fatigue I did not get it: Tim was a sort of lover and accessory to the collector's life, but when this tour was over, he, too, would be ejected. He did

1. Of Hale, Noguchi once said, "She was a beautiful girl. All of my girls are beautiful."

115

seem to believe that he was convincing me regarding how welcome he was as we trailed upstairs and down, past custom cabinetry, but in truth he was doing the opposite. I feared for Tim in this vast, high place.

I didn't tell Tim this because I never tell Tim anything. (What would be the point?) Instead, once the inevitable took hold and we were both back out on the sidewalk, I declined drinks with him, citing a date with an ex that was actual and which I had made months in advance and expressly in order to avoid these very drinks.

My ex's name was Francis, and these days he was married to a high-powered person and had multiple kids. The high-powered person's executive status allowed Francis to style his sweatpants and cardigan with a certain flair. And who am I kidding: it wasn't "a certain flair." Francis looked fantastic, comfy, loose. He twirled his macaroni and yarn necklace. Life was good.

Francis's phone was even broken. By this I mean, the screen was smashed, the storage full, and it could no longer be updated. It was an amber-frozen bug, mostly used for texting.

Nevertheless, Francis had it out.

He flipped through some pictures of his babies.

There were three of them and their pink faces were often in the grass or sky.

The phone had to be shaken, the JPEGs enlarged, dragged, due to obstruction caused by jagged cracks and duct tape, but I thought I was mostly seeing everything. It must be amazing, I thought, to have just one life, with people dependent on you in it, with whom you do not communicate primarily by email, invoice, or oblique threat.

Francis, for his part, watched me. If somebody was crying, he swooped in, moved hastily past that photo.

In a gesture I assumed would be futile but which I was going to try out anyway, I decided to display the abstract nature of my own existence.

"I just remembered!" I exclaimed.

"Yeah?" said Francis. I had interrupted him.

"Yeah," I said. "This was so funny." And on my own pristine phone I caused to surface an image. This image, I believed, was sort of perfect.

I surrendered the device, along with the perfect image, to Francis.

"Oh," said Francis, now looking at the perfect image. "Wow." And then: "What is that?"

The photograph he was looking at was free of people. It was free of everything save for a VHS cassette tape case, and on this VHS cassette tape case was a title, presumably of the tape's contents. The title read: *The Care Bears Find and Kill God*. Below the title were some Care Bears stomping around on a puffy cloud. Obviously, it wasn't real.

"It's a joke," I said idiotically.

"No, it's so funny," Francis reassured me, helplessly repeating my own phrase. "Is that something you made?"

Here Francis made reference to my early ambition to be-come an artist.

"Oh, I just saw it," I told him.

Francis diligently returned the phone. "It's so clean," he was saying, in reference, I have to assume, to the appliance.

Anyway, I was only thinking, as I always did in these moments, of the death of god at the hands/paws of the Care Bears. One had to believe god never saw it coming, that in his infinite wisdom he had somehow neglected to foresee that cartoon avatars created by his own most troublesome creations (humans) would someday transcend the temporal, spatial, and material limits of the universe in order to find out where he lived and then go to where he lived and slay him. You had to imagine god coming to open the door, prob-ably still in his apron, wiping his wet hands off on the back of his jeans, like, "Just a goddamn second!" Maybe, in spite of taking his own name in vain, he was actually having a pretty good day.

I also thought of the determination of the Care Bears. It's quite a thing to unpeel all the layers of philosophy, the-ology, and physics in order to find that address. This is to say nothing of actually going there—and then, like, killing somebody.

I wondered if this meant that we were all Care Bears. Or if we could become Care Bears, if we tried hard enough and cared enough and did extremely well. The title announced a documentary event that would occur before your very eyes if you watched this tape; the title announced that, actually, this event had already occurred, and god was dead, and an ursine clique had done it.

Their scented clouds, their vapor car, their thematic stomachs . . .

Francis, who was polite, started asking me about my day.

And I wanted to tell Francis about what I had seen. I wanted to tell Francis that I had encountered a person who was adjacent to, and who perhaps encountered on a repeating basis, the rulers of our world. I wanted to say that I had seen her terrible, beautiful, stupid study room, with its ungodly chaise upholstered in white fur, with figured legs of leaded crystal. I wanted to let him know how I had been invited to sit down on this gleaming, terrifying article and how a priceless book had been set before me. And how I had touched the book, much as I touched the fur, and how, as they had watched me and breathed upon my neck, I had said a word that isn't a word, "Wow." "Wow, wow, wow," I said. And how I said the word "this," which isn't a word, either, once you say it enough. "This," I said. How I said: "This! This!" And how I was tired, so tired there, in the mist of my false awe, and how I was tired, too, talking to lucky Francis, and so I said, "It was pretty good."

Bitter Tennis

I go to visit Jon on the A. It's a straight shot but I'm late. I sit in one of the two-seat sections, between a door and the front of the train. I am reading Jon's story on my phone. Occasionally, a text drops down, obscuring the top of the PDF. The messages are all from the same person. I will be meeting this person for dinner later this evening. We'll be having sex after we have dinner. All this is certain. The person texting me is my closest friend. Jon is just a professional friend and I'm going to see him for work. I am his editor. I should have read his story earlier. I'm at the point where I'm so exhausted this spring I haven't even bothered to dress in an appealing way. It's so unseasonably cold and I know Jon wants to sit outside. I'm wearing a long black wool coat and bright blue running sneakers. The sneakers have orange treads. I am carrying the smallest bag I can get away with, which has a metal chain and leather strap, but not the kind you're thinking of. It takes too much energy to describe the look I'm going for, but it has to do with trying to look like I do not care, which, in this rather unique instance, is even slightly true. I do not care much, although my heart is racing, and somehow I want everyone to know.

I live at the bottom of the ocean. I am capable of quick motion but do not warm. I cause my eyes to grasp each of Jon's words. I live among the bristlemouths, the viperfish, the anglerfish, the cookiecutter sharks, the eelpouts. I don't know why Jon and I can't just have this conversation over the phone.

The A train is moving as efficiently as one could wish, but I know that I am going to be late. Across from me are two teenage girls who are rapidly becoming the heroes of this trip. They are tough and impeccably dressed. One of them causes a fidget spinner to spin. They are talking about alcohol. They do some work on their phones then conscientiously put the phones away. They focus on each other; the one girl, the taller, the prettier one, manipulates a black and gold fidget spinner. I swoon for them. I imagine they will move to Los Angeles at some point because there is nowhere in New York for them to live now. They cannot go to Prospect Heights with its Ivy-educated transplants, and they can't stay home with their parents in Inwood. They can't live in Bushwick—they might sublet there a few months but it won't last—and they can't join a Ridgewood commune. Chinatown is too expensive. Williamsburg overrun by Europeans. For these reasons, there is nowhere to go and they must become Angelinos. One of them will make a lot of money. One will have kids. They are placid and gorgeous and discussing how they will obtain what sounds like gin. It's so innocent and here they are criticizing someone but it's fair, I tell you. It is very fair. I can tell.

I move my eyes back onto Jon's story. A text drops down. "Do you want to just meet there," my friend wants to know. Then my friend sends a link to something on Twitter. I will read these messages in situ later. I absolutely will not click on the Twitter link, I tell myself, as I click through to an image of a tiny black cat whose highly visible pink tongue extends from its all but invisible mouth. I try to think of what I will say in response to this vision. I often write, in response to such links from my friend, "It doesn't like that," by which I indicate that the animal doesn't want to be photographed and thereby rendered semi-humanoid as well as the punch line of somebody's not particularly excellent joke. I also mean that the animal doesn't like being conveyed to me as a Twitter link. The animal would ideally like to appear to me as its IRL self, corporeal and gleaming, speaking its own strange language. And what I therefore *also* mean is, much as the animal desires physical proximity to me, so does my friend. He cannot hide his desire, not with all the Twitter links in the world. I'm teasing, of course, when I send my set phrase, but at the same time I am not teasing, not at all. "It doesn't like that," I type. Is there part of me that wants to shout, to yell uncontrollably, YOU CANNOT HIDE? Yes, there must be. Because, in fact, you cannot hide. Not from me. I'll tell you that right now. I'm a very good reader. Although I seldom mention this to anyone I know.

I live at the bottom of the ocean and Jon wants to play tennis. It's why I have to travel so far. I mean, Jon doesn't actually want me to play tennis, but he wants me to meet him at the tennis center at the top of Manhattan where he takes his daughter for her tennis lessons and he wants to tell me, while I am there, that he would like me to play tennis with him.

Clearly, this means something.

There was a time when I myself was a daughter who took tennis lessons, and I've apprised Jon of this fact. Therefore Jon is trying, in some sense, to match up our respective familial situations. He's thinking, you did that and I do this—therefore perhaps it's a good idea for us to meet in the middle of this piece of coincidence, so we can both try to figure out if there's any useful information in it. In other words, Jon thinks we have stuff in common. And since we work together and since Jon writes a lot of memoir, he's multitasking. He's doing research for a new piece—probably a whole book about tennis—at the same time as he is revising something he wrote three years ago.

He also doesn't seem to mind that I'm forty minutes late.

"You're here!" he cries.

We're both surprised. I'm used to meeting him in the usual places where editors meet their writers. I encounter him over email, at parties, in fancy bars. I salute him in passing on social media. We're privy to some of the same artisanal gossip mills.

But here we are beneath fluorescent lights in a reception area straight out of 1980-something. I have, suddenly, a memory of what it was like to be a child in the 1980s, when I was the small charge of upwardly mobile parents. What's really strange is that this setting causes me to recall what it was like to be innocent—at least, for a second I think it does.

Jon, meanwhile, wants to know if I'd like to see the courts.

"Sure," I tell him. I express some vague concern about being an unauthorized visitor, treading on hallowed athletic ground, but he brushes it off. "I *did* wear sneakers," I volunteer, as if this was clever of me.

"Did you read the story?" Jon asks. He's leading me into the bubble. The sounds of tennis—pops and little cries—are apparent.

"Yes," I both lie and do not lie. "It's looking good," I say, which is a guess more than anything.

Jon doesn't reply. He nods toward the court where his lanky daughter is demolishing a boy who looks to be a year or two older than she is.

At a pause in play, the daughter seeks Jon out. Her face is radiant. She waves enthusiastically.

"I have some beer," Jon offers. "Let's go outside." He is laughing and waving back at his daughter at the same time as he says this. The pairing is incongruous and therefore extremely impressive.

Jon, I think, has a full life.

Jon goes into a duffle he's stashed in the bleachers and pulls out a pair of bottles. "OK," he says, laughing again. He's leading me back out. "They're warm."

I have to rush to keep up with Jon. He's more than twenty years my senior, but he does seem to have some kind of incredible physical advantage.

"(."

Or I mean, *Open parenthesis.* Or, Speak now, memory. I mean, I have to pause for a moment here because I want to tell you something about myself before we get to the matter of Jon and his prose and what we say to each other once we're outside the tennis bubble. I'm somewhat repressed— or "reserved," as my friend Andrew once put it—and it does take a certain amount of energy to exit the gravitational field of the present. All I seem to be able to come up with at the moment isn't even a memory but rather a story I once read in an extremely famous book, but if we pretend that it's a story I myself made up, a story somehow about me, then we'll get somewhere, I hope. By which I mean, to the bottom of the ocean. Where, as mentioned, I happen to live.

Here is the story: Imagine that you have died (weird), and after your death you awake into what is apparently another world. You aren't sure if or how this world is connected to the world you inhabited while you were alive, but you are pretty sure that you can't return to the place you lived while you were living by simply walking around. Meanwhile, it turns out that you are no longer a body. You're a soul. You find yourself on a shoreline made of clean, gray ash. There is water sitting hazily in a great expanse before you. You can barely hear anything.

You realize that you are not the only soul here. There are countless other souls hovering in this place, gazing out across the water.

Then you realize that there are lives here, too. Not just souls. You're not going to be stuck here. All along the shoreline sit countless lives in the bank of clean ash. You're not a life, you're a soul, but you can see them, the lives, and you know something about what they are. It's difficult to describe how the lives look, but maybe it's enough to say they look like sticks of different sizes, cut from saplings, although there are no trees anywhere around.

You begin to examine the different lives. There are so

many. The soul must choose. It has to live eventually, but it does not have to live a life it does not select. And so the soul searches, and it lands.

As this ancient story purports to show, everyone has, at some level, chosen the life they live. The story also claims—leaving out the reincarnation bit, which I don't care as much about—that none of us could avoid choosing. And this is what I want you to understand, regarding me: I'm trying to figure out what to do in a scenario in which I have no choice but, at some bare minimum, to keep on existing.

I don't feel free. Moreover, I feel kind of scared.

I think, by the way, returning to sports, that the way my father dealt with this problem was to play tennis. Because, to be clear, having chosen to be male does not exempt one from the difficulties! I know I'm getting ahead of myself and it's just a conjecture, but let me keep going: I think that my father decided to teach himself tennis for a bunch of different reasons, in part to obscure his working-class origins and in part to have virtuous reasons to exit the house. But these are probably only the reasons he was conscious of. Much as, if the story about souls recounted here is plausible, if not actually true—and there are aspects of everything we do that we have not chosen for ourselves, not in so many words, even as we *have* chosen them—then my father's choice of tennis as one of his main physical and creative outlets in life came at a cost. It was a form of leisure for him but, given his broader cosmological setup, did not mean that he was either free or having fun.

I don't know much about the cosmos, but I know enough to avoid the game of tennis.

Close parenthesis.

Jon and I are sitting together outside the bubble. There's a bench here, plus gravel. Below us, near the water, reeds and cattails grow. Jon has already freaked me out by insisting on going inside to the reception desk to ask for a bottle opener, an act I find brazen in the extreme, given that what we're doing out here with our beers is almost certainly illegal.

Jon keeps laughing at me, but about some things he is deadly earnest. "So what did you think of the story?" he persists. At this moment both of us happen to be staring at a giant blue word, COLUMBIA, painted on a cliff. I realize that Jon plays his tennis here because he is an alumnus.

"It's good," I say. "I really like it."

"Right," Jon says, "but do you think it needs a little more, a little less? I think you were correct about the androids needing to go. I haven't really done enough research on that. I got a little too excited when I saw that *Times* article."

I try to reassure Jon that although I suggested cutting the android part, it was still pretty good. I tell him that maybe he should devote a whole story to androids.

"A whole story on androids? I don't know about that." Jon takes a sip from his beer. He clears his throat, and I can tell he is about to say something he considers important. "I really like writing about androids but more as a way to think about people, you know? I don't care about the immortal soul but, you know, some of my readers *do*."

Jon is laughing again.

"Sure," I start to say. I'm about to explain to Jon that this was not what I meant, but he interrupts me:

"It just wouldn't work. I never want to have a story that's about one thing."

"But you're so good at description!" I exclaim. I'm trying to say that I think Jon can write about whatever he wants. There's a lot he can get away with.

"Thank you. But I'm never going to write about androids. They have to be a side issue. You know, there was something else that seems relevant, I'm just trying to remember. Oh, yeah."

And Jon tells me the following story:

When Jon was in grad school, he spent a lot of time observing people. He wasn't a bad student, exactly, but he was studying literature and one of the things he knew about literature was that he himself could write it, and this fact troubled his relationship to scholarship, as such. Literature, as everyone knows, is a massive info leak, while scholarship mostly purports to reveal helpful stuff people really *ought* to know, and all Jon wanted to do while he was obtaining his degree was to give away destabilizing secrets regarding academia. This desire made it difficult to concentrate, among other difficulties. Jon got very interested in sociology, as well as cybernetics. He liked vaguely paranoid theories based on the schematization of the social sphere. He enjoyed thinking about what computing had to do with anything, partly perversely, because in spite of Apple's bombastic presence on the home electronics scene since that 1984 Super Bowl commercial, few people in the humanities were bothering to think about what effect their word processing and emailing were having on their knowledge. Jon, by contrast, was brilliant and somewhat young.

But these, as Jon might say, are side issues. They're just here to give us some sense of what Jon was like. In fact, he was pretty similar then to the person he is now, except that he was unmarried and did not have a daughter.

Also Jon had to take classes for a few years, and because of this he came into contact with other students. Among these people was a certain young woman, who is the person of interest as far as Jon's story is concerned.

This young woman had a problem. It was a problem that interested Jon, given his social-scientific explorations, because it both was and was not her problem. The young woman's problem was that she was not recognizable. It wasn't, for example, that she was invisible or that she shrank from human contact—far from it. In Jon's account, she was more than reasonably attractive, always simply and elegantly dressed. She had a nice face, nice hair. She spoke with an amount of self-assurance that was neither excessive nor too puny. No, the young woman was perfectly visible and in no particular way repulsive, but nevertheless this did not prevent her from being largely unrecognizable in the eyes of others.

Graduate school, it seems, is an interesting setting in which to observe such a problem play out. The reason for this is that graduate school, particularly in the humanities, is where people go to learn how to introduce themselves. This is perhaps the main skill taught to students of the humanities. The lesson was long and particularly difficult for the young woman who was not recognizable, because she was constantly having to reintroduce herself everywhere she went. For Jon it became a kind of private running joke, although one he did not dare to share with the woman herself. Whenever they were in class together, he would wait for the inevitable moment at which the professor would squint or point and ask, "And *who* are you?" only to be reminded that the student in question had already been known to him or her for multiple weeks, months, and even years.

Somehow, the reminding did not serve to reinforce

memory regarding the unrecognizable student. It was as if she suffered from a detachable aphasia, an amnesia she herself did not possess. It interested Jon for, as he put it, two main reasons: One, this was a psychosocial malady affecting a single organism that seemed to have come into being outside that organism's body (and truly it was difficult to say if the problem originated with the woman or with others). Two, this was a malady to which Jon seemed, among all his peers and overlords, to be the sole person who was immune.

Jon could recognize the woman.

It was surprising and even semi-miraculous.

At first Jon could barely believe it.

Months went by, maybe a full semester, and at last Jon got up the courage to speak to the woman, with whom, if this is not already obvious, he had managed to fall deeply in love. It was not at all a difficult thing to speak to her. They went out together to a late lunch of desserts and talked a long time.

It was also surprisingly easy to avoid the "recognition issue." There was a nearly otherworldly quality to the woman, in that she herself seemed completely unaware that most other people never had any idea who she was. She lived, oblivious to the problem, and she was even happy.

Jon courted her carefully. In spite of their mutual penury, they went out to many meals and talked many long talks. Jon believed that he had discovered a previously unknown plane of existence. His studies took on new meaning.

But when summer came again, the woman departed for the West Coast. This was years before the tech bubble burst, a fact that dates Jon a bit, and it seemed like someone had made the woman an offer she couldn't refuse.

Jon wanted to go with her, but the woman wasn't interested. She said something incomprehensible—to Jon, at least—about how her decision had to do with wanting to live a different sort of life. She told Jon that he knew her too well.

"You should write that down," I tell Jon, when he is done.

"Maybe I will." He barely pauses. "When do you think the current story is going to come out?"

"Soon," I say. I mention that there are two other editors who are reading it, who are perhaps a little less attentive to Jon than I am. I tell Jon I'll bug them, and that he should bug them, too.

"OK," Jon says. Then, "Don't you have any questions?"

"Questions?"

"About the story."

"Oh," I say. "I thought the whole point of this meeting was to come to a consensus about that."

"No," says Jon. "I mean the story I just told you." He finishes his beer. "Don't you have any questions about that?"

I have to think for a minute. "Well," I say, "do you know what happened to her?"

"So you assume the story is true."

"Isn't it?"

"I don't know if that matters," Jon says. "But yeah. I've been looking for her on Facebook. My sense is she's been rather successful."

"Oh," I say.

"She was kind of a writer. Maybe half a writer? I don't know. The one really strange thing about her, aside from the unrecognizability thing, of course, was how much she liked puns. If I'd been thinking about it more clearly I could have seen the end coming."

"The lowest form of humor," I say, skirting Jon's reference to pain.

"Obviously I couldn't take the joke."

It's beginning to get dark and I find myself staring extra hard at the Columbia insignia on the cliff across from us. It stays clear and distinct, even as everything else around us dims to a blue mush. For a while, both Jon and I stop making an effort to speak.

Then Jon says, "You know there's a reason I'm telling you this story."

"There always is." I mean it in a nice way.

Jon is not listening. He says, "It's a circumstantial reason. It's because of tennis. I was in the bookstore the other day, browsing for things about your tennis game, you know, as one does, and, I mean, it's not a thing I would do, read a tennis book, but I was down there in Sports, and I swear, out of the corner of my eye, I thought I saw something called Bitter Tennis, which is a great title, right?"

"A fantastic title," I say.

"I know. But of course it was a misreading. But this was when, after all these years, I think I understood."

I don't say anything.

"This was why she had to leave. Everyone was just taking things so psychotically literally!" Jon chuckles. He tugs at the lobe of his right ear.

I say, "Is this a real person?"

"Let's go indoors," Jon tells me. "I have to check if the match is done."

"You remembered that," I say, as I attempt to hide my mostly empty beer bottle in the pocket of my coat. The bottle protrudes but not, I think, too alarmingly.

"Remembered what?" Jon is climbing the small hill of the patio.

For a second I'm confused and don't know what to say. For a second I genuinely feel as if I don't know or can't remember what I'm referring to. The reception area before us is brightly lit, and through the large window I can perceive a huddle of youngish professional men who have arrived to play tennis together. A few of them are wearing white terry-cloth headbands in an un-ironic way. They stand around the sofas, stretching, fiddling with racquet strings and expensive leather attachés.

But I recover. I sense a sort of infinite laugh rising in me, and instead of laughing I keep talking. I say, "The pun. *Bitter Tennis*. You remembered."

"Memory is funny, too," says Jon. "Here," he says, when we are indoors. "Give me your beer," and he throws the illicit bottle away for me, indicating, unexpectedly, that he understands how uncomfortable I feel.

I have the impression that all the tennis players in the reception area are staring at us. I want to keep things brief. "It was nice talking," I tell Jon.

"Indeed."

"I'm just going to use the restroom."

"Do you feel like a quick game? I noticed that you're wearing sneakers. I have extra racquets. We can find your size."

"I can't," I say. "I have to meet someone for dinner."

Jon laughs. He really seems to be in a great mood, in spite of the story. Or maybe it's the story that's making him happy, who knows. It clearly means something to him that I've come all the way up here.

"I guess you're going, then?"

"I am."

"Well, let me know about the story?"

I think he means the one that he's already written, and I tell Jon that I will. Jon is a fantastic human. I feel less afraid of the wealthy tennis players and their irony deficiency and go to use the women's restroom.

My phone, meanwhile, makes a noise. It's my friend.

"It does like that," he writes.

A gray thought bubble with an animated ellipsis indicates that he is, wherever he is, continuing to type.

I silence the phone and take my time urinating. I wash my hands and examine my hair. Everything about me seems reasonable. It's spring and my freckles are coming out.

On the way to the subway, I look at my phone again. A new message has appeared.

"It likes that very much," my friend confidently opines.

I switch the sound on but then turn the phone off. I feel weak but satisfied. It has been a good meeting.

I can remember there was—and this is a true story—one afternoon when, freshly returned from his habitual tennis game and having consumed half a beer, my father threatened to kill me. I was possibly twenty on the day in question and this time he was serious, although I suppose that hardly matters. I used to lock my door whenever I was alone in the house with him. Mentally, I'd call it dehydration. My mother would begin laughing wildly if I tried to recount these sorts of events. "Your father loves you," she liked to say, but she didn't need to be out of earshot for my father to begin talking about which random women in the news it was he presently wanted to assault, whose voices were the most whiny, the most beset by vocal fry.

This is why I moved to the bottom of the ocean. I packed a suitcase long ago. You might think this is a sad thing, but I've come to enjoy the incoherent ministrations of the sub-photic beings of the hadal zone, their telescopic eyes and spiny or gelatinous skin. I like the suborder Ceratioidei. I have no idea what they're saying when their fanged mouths move, but I can always use my phone if I get too hard up for fellowship.

The other nice thing about my current trench community is that it's pretty dense. We are, speaking of puns, under a great deal of pressure, but here, and maybe only here, there's no such thing as tennis.

Louise Nevelson

Among my mother's twenty-three friends on Facebook are my ex-husband and my mother's former best friend, Max. I am not on speaking terms with either of these individuals and neither, I hope, is my mother. My former husband was living a double life for the last three years of our union and Max, my mother's former best friend, is dead. Of these unfortunate circumstances my mother and I say exactly nothing. There are one or two people who regularly "like" my mother's posts. I am not among them.

Max seems to have been an OK person. My mother met her recently, within the last decade, and there are a total of four details I can recall regarding the life of Max:

1. Max had an adult son who was a classical musician (I do not recall his instrument)

2. Max was a woman artist who had a family
    instead of a career
3. Max and my mother occasionally com-
    muned in nature in Connecticut where
    both Max and her second husband and my
    mother and my father, who is my mother's
    first husband, have second homes
4. Max died swiftly of terminal cancer (I do
    not recall which kind)

I became aware of the last of these details by way of an art object that appeared in the living room of my parents' second home. The home has an open floor plan on the second floor and the art object had been given pride of place. It stood on an antique chest (scrolling ribbon work and elaborate lock) at the top of the stairs. Attaining the second floor you met the gaze of the object's numerous intriguingly drilled orifices, its segmented wooden arm, its awkward pareidolic splendor. The object appeared to be tooting. It was stiffly, silently tooting and motionlessly marching and pointing all over the room. It was a masterwork of late modernism, partaking of a style definitively and exhaustively explored by the artist Louise Nevelson. The art object, which was admittedly all but silently shouting that it recognized and pretty well comprehended that it was a rip-off of a Louise Nevelson, was painted a not entirely unappealing terra-cotta rose. It was a little less than two feet tall. It stood before a window facing south.

When I first saw this object I carefully indicated to my mother its resemblance to the work of Louise Nevelson. I attempted to proceed with tact. I gingerly inched out of the shadows, choosing my words with care, wanting to know, did my mother suspect that there might be any way Max had been at all familiar?

"I got that out of her garage," my mother said. We were going to have dinner in fifteen minutes. The open floor plan meant that views of the kitchen with its steaming pasta pot were available. My father had dropped off to sleep on the sectional.

Because I still thought this was a joke, this willing selection of an obviously derivative kitsch item, I suggested, "It *spoke* to you?"

My mother continued, "After Max died her husband, really *sweet* guy"—this pronounced with no feeling—"said I could take something. She had a studio."

"Oh," I said, as a veil brushed sleepily across the room. "She's dead?"

"Yes," my mother said. "Just like Louise Nevelson."

There has always been a lot of math going on around me, and lately I am learning more about it. For example, my mother has recently been playing more and more tennis, despite her dislike of the sport. She does so because my father's tennis game has been growing increasingly weak, due to his age (seventy-seven), and because tennis was my father's one great love in life. It is unclear, in this sense, whether my mother is somehow acting as a bridge between my father and his one great love, the game of tennis, or if, in a continuation of other questionable behavior on her part, she is quietly robbing him of his most private joy. That my mother has also used my father's love of tennis as at once a cloak and rationale for her infidelities complicates the story, or, rather, the math, of which, as I have mentioned, there has been a lot.

Also complicating our math is the fact that my mother, unlike my father, has no great loves. This is the math that the shameful fail to see: Those who feel no shame can also feel no love. They may feel other things, but love is absolutely denied them. This is why shame, not tragic fate, is the other—the double and/or opposite—of luck. Those who are capable of shame are also capable of much else.

My mother, although shameless, understands this math. This is why she has had to do so very much in order, as she puts it, "to survive."

I, meanwhile, am my mother's large adult child.

I use this language partly in jest. You will find it on the Internet. People say (i.e., type), "large adult son." They mean something has gone wrong. They mean that an adult son is still around, lingering for ease of comparison. There is another meme I consider nominally related. The text is something like, "Don't talk to me or my son ever again." The idea is schoolyard or mall or parking lot as libidinal zone, the awkwardness of attachment, how it looks like Dad is wearing an invisible apron as he stiffly shields his offspring from some important villain. Once I saw someone caption an image of a large Perrier bottle beside a small Perrier bottle with this text. That was outstanding.

I am my mother's large adult daughter. I am not really that large, and I am not even particularly adult. I can, in theory, for example, bear children for several years to come, which for a woman means, I believe, that she is still quite young.

Regarding the meme invoked above, re: talking and sons, I am not entirely sure what my mother is trying to protect me from. My mother from time to time comments on my youth in an abashed way. "You are *so* young!" she whispers, touching her own face. "Your skin," she murmurs, stroking her hair. Yet I do my own taxes, indicating, by way of contrast, my relative lack of naïveté.

Several years ago, long before Max's death, my mother recounted a nightmare she had had about Connecticut. In the nightmare, my father was dead, and my mother was forced to live "in town." She said that in the nightmare she did not own a car because she could not afford one and was forced to walk, on the actual sidewalk, to the actual grocery store. My mother said that she was alone in the house "in town" and had to attempt to save money, an undertaking she found extremely frightening. My mother told me this as she drove.

My father, who does not really speak to me, was asleep in the backseat.

These are a very few of the extremely few scenes I am able to relate from the long-term standoff that constitutes my primary human relationship.

Louise Nevelson, after whose art my mother's friend Max shamelessly styled her own, was an American sculptor. Louise Nevelson lived for nearly a century, from 1899 to 1988. She was born in the ancient city of Pereiaslav-Khmelnytskyi, formerly Pereyaslav, in central Ukraine. In 1897, there were some ten thousand Jewish persons living in Pereyaslav. In 2017, there are fewer than a hundred in Pereiaslav-Khmelnytskyi, which is renowned for its museums.

Louise Nevelson's paternal grandfather was a dealer in wood. Nevelson's father, Isaac Berliawsky, was a merchant who emigrated to America in 1902, sending for his wife and children three years later. Nevelson's best-known works are monumental wooden sculptures painted a single color, usually black or white. To my eye, they appear charred.

Louise Nevelson is associated with such American artists as Robert Rauschenberg and Jasper Johns. It is said that Nevelson began working with wood during the late 1930s when, impoverished, she and her son wandered the streets of

New York looking for scraps to burn. Her son later became a sculptor.

Like Louise Nevelson, Max gave birth to a son who became an artist. Unlike Louise Nevelson's son, Max's son is better known for his art than his mother was for hers. Louise Nevelson identified strongly with her father, at least as far as her professional life was concerned, and her relationship with her son was always strained. Max, on the other hand, understood motherhood as a surpassing achievement, although she had a first name that might, sight unseen, allow her to be mistaken for a man.

Ah, gender! How you have continued, in spite of the optimistic tidings of my middle school teachers, to be a pressing concern! Truly, it is a remarkable thing, how thoroughly my life has been defined by my female status. It is worse now even than it was when I was eleven, when I was sixteen, when I was twenty-five, because now I understand the social differentiation of sex. I feel as if I am crouched over in permanence, waiting out my biological clock, praying that the stroke of midnight will unsex me, to use Lady Macbeth's helpfully plain verb, although I know that it will not. No matter how old I become, it will always have been possible for me to have "had" children. The infinitesimal lessening of onus here constitutes a pillar of women's liberation, so called.

I am one of the animals. I live among the other human

animals and am one of them. Nothing animal is outlandish to me.

My mother, who never comments on the early termination of my marriage, has always had things to say regarding the project of becoming an artist. Although she has had a number of friends who were artists, even before the advent of Max, most of her artist-related pronouncements are not very nice. Artists are poor and unrecognized. Society mocks them. Artists are deluded by the success of a small number of artists who arbitrarily meet with forms of reward that have no intrinsic or necessary relationship to the objects they produce. Everything in the project of art-making is hazard and/or luck and/or prostitution. Those who labor on in obscurity do so at risk of madness. Their lives are unsanitary.

The not-insignificant irony of this particular aesthetic theory is that my mother is herself a pretty creative type. I would not go so far as to call her an artist, but she *is* a talented liar.

I wish now to discuss with you my mother's great artistic feat in life, the work that has for so long consumed her. I wish also to discuss the impact of her great feat on me. I am part of my mother's great feat, although my role is but a supporting one, if not that of an *infans* extra. I am a part of my mother's masterpiece, if distantly. I stand before it, and

I tremble. I fear it more than solitude plus genteel penury in any Connecticut town.

This is to say that, unable to resist the siren song of symmetry, a.k.a. the math, a.k.a. the vibrating abyss and/or much-doctored scorecard that is our family, my mother invited her lover to the release event for the publication of my latest novel. It took me a couple of weeks to figure out that this had occurred, the appearance of the lover, I mean. The lover is, unlike my mother's friend Max, not dead and, in fact, when I think about it, probably he looks more vital than ever. I saw him but did not quite see him there. I learned who he was through another friend, who once held a subordinate position in the workplace where for many years my mother was an important individual.

"Oh," the friend said to me, looking up out of her beer, "so-and-so was at your reading. He was lurking at the back. Remember how years ago he took me to that Bob Dylan concert? I thought that was so inappropriate." I was nodding to her because I could remember. "I remember," my friend said, "because he was there that weekend with his much younger girlfriend and later I heard his wife sing at the funeral for—." My friend was continuing to speak. She was explaining how so-and-so, my mother's former colleague and, we all believe, her lover was unfaithful to everyone he knew, not just his wife, his younger girlfriend, or, for that matter, my mother. And so-and-so stood at the back of the reading for my new novel, too. So-and-so was ancient and handsome and living and did not attempt to speak to me. He was probably younger than he'd ever been.

My father, meanwhile, sat there. My father did not even glance at the back of the room. He was holding a guide to better tennis.

Trust

I meet the artist, who does x, for a snack one afternoon. We have the kind of conversation it was more necessary to have previous to the existence of the Internet. We exchange general info about the world.

I am attempting to experience a feeling of warmth. It's general, too. The artist who does x is commenting on the method by which thermostat fixtures have been incorporated into the bakery's wall décor. She expresses amazement. Possibly she's struggling.

I cannot remember if the artist who does x says that we should do this again. She offers a few tips for improved existence, evidently intending that I remember and deploy these in a eulogy, should I, at her expiration, have acquired sufficient cultural capital to merit a speaker's invitation to the funeral.

In this fantasy, she is buried in state.

Why, I ask myself, are so many of the artist who does x's thoughts about what will happen after one, or both, of us goes away? Why do I understand this so well?

It's true I've been thinking about writing out a list of all my enemies, including brief descriptions of their unique powers and weaknesses. The artist who does x would not appear on this list—and is very unlikely to appear on any subsequent lists of this type—but her behavior suggests that she is concerned about the possibility of a public airing of such a document. For in her mind, she may well have made it. In this fantasy, she lives forever and suffers eternally under the tip of my poison pen. I see she wants to be ready, should it come to pass that my list is aired and she is at the top, number one, where permanent marker forms an escutcheon of loathing. Arrows point! Emphatic asterisks! Random flowers! Stars. "She is the worst!" my list might say.

And yet it doesn't.

How can the artist who does x not know? How can she not tell that I have no intention of putting her on the list of "Folks I'd Like to <u>KILL</u>" today, next week, or ever, really? We're just meeting at a mediocre bakery in Chelsea. I'm listening to her talk about her life.

It should, by the way, be obvious that I am not an artist. And it would be nice if everyone I know recognized this, yet no one does. I have the opposite problem of almost everybody in this industry. Everyone has been calling me a closet conceptualist and "mail artist" and performance artist of institutional critique and a post-Internet artworker since day one of my career in gallery admin, but really what I am is a person who, for various complex and private reasons, mainly feels comfortable with menial tasks and who is, meanwhile, of above-average intelligence. If these facts alone make me an artist, then, fine, so be it, I am an artist, but I kindly request that somebody for once concede that this is probably not the case. I do not make art. I do not have a personal website. I do keep my desk neat, which some passersby term art. I use adjectives in email. I don't own many clothes. I am tall and thin and speak softly.

I'm also significantly younger than the artist who does x, although I've already aged out of my current position at the gallery. Indeed, my current position is not a career and is not intended for individuals of my advanced age (thirty-one). Luckily, as I have no dependents or other prospects, I'm allowed to stay on. I've been told I save them the trouble of training a third intern. But since I'm the one who does said training and spends a great deal of her time emailing with, and identifying the clerical errors of, said interns, I'm not sure what this means. I like to think it means that I've been fully absorbed, that I'm irreplaceably part of the gallery's vital human architecture, but I know that come the next financial crisis, the first pink slip, written haltingly out in shaky Japanese felt tip and not without tears, shall be mine.

In this sense, my friendship with the artist who does x, who is represented by the gallery, is either a piece of professional security with which I am padding my impending fall, or it is emotional labor the gallery farms out to me because it can reasonably be assumed that I am someone for whom a friendship with the artist who does x has its advantages.

I don't love these alternatives.

Meanwhile, the artist who does x and I exit the bakery.

We're done snacking.

She looks elated that we've made it out of confined quarters and are soon to be free of each other. I study this in her, along with her expensive hat. She has begun telling a story I realize, with a sharp slide into nausea, is inappropriately long given the impending leave-taking, the timing of crosswalk signals, not to mention her already apparent wish to be out of my presence.

"Years ago," begins the artist who does x, "I was working on a poster installation. It was during my minimal era when I was trying not to do anything, when I was trying not to make art, you know? I wanted to be something else, then. I wanted to be anything but an artist, and I was under the impression that if I did little enough, if I did barely enough, the world would just let me go. And maybe I was even a little angry about that possibility? Of being disposable? And so I had these posters, and they weren't even *of* anything, they were these bad images I had taken of other posters, at the movies, or the hairdresser's, for shows and things. But of course you know what I am talking about already, you know this was 'Limelight,' and actually when you look back this was what made me, not in that sense of some blue-chip fantasy of fame, but this was the time I did the thing that was *me*, that said *me* more than anything before, that wasn't an imitation of some hero of mine and wasn't me attempting to do what I thought everyone else wanted and it only happened because I did it, and I was so angry at that time, and so fed up, and so, or so I thought, beyond anything at all, I was feeling, what was the point? However this was what I did and it worked so fucking well I was able to work for the rest of my life, which, as you know, I have. It's a miracle. It's so funny that it came out of this moment of truly *intense* self-loathing. I wonder if you can understand that. But the other night I was lying in bed at home, in my country home, it's quite quiet there, you know, you can really hear things, and I have this sky-light. It's not directly above the bed, but I can see it, and I can see whatever light comes through, and I like to think about, *well*, what might be going on in the sky, and I thought about what might be located there because others have seen it, what could possibly be there *just* because others have seen it, you know? Others who have lain awake looking? Oh, it's impossible, of course; of course there's nothing. It's just an idea I'm having and probably you're late, Justine, yes? You need to get back? No? You have a minute? Well, I was lying there, looking at this sky I could not see, or thinking about *actually* looking at a kind of sky that does not exist, one that bears, in itself, all the insignificant marks, the ashes and the contrails, the frothy little wakes, the flecks and pits, from the looking, you know, all that looking that's got to be so impure! And that's what I've *always* been thinking about in my work, I realized, the way a thing *looks* because it's been looked at, the way a place looks, how it's changed—and that's, you know, that's what's got me thinking about the sky. Is there anything else in the world that's been, you know, *so* looked at?

"I didn't want to get out of bed. It wasn't that I wanted to go see the sky. I just wanted to be able to hold it in my mind, this idea, of this sky, this version of the sky—that there was something that was so obviously there, but that you couldn't see—that I couldn't see. It was, if you'll forgive me saying this—I don't know what this even means these days—it was like trust—not feeling it, you know, because actually I seldom feel it? But it was like the notion of trust, which has always been in my life if somewhat out of reach—and for me it is, and perhaps this is part of the problem if not the simple strangeness of it. Trust is like an image and I am forever trying to see it. I can feel the outlines of it, you know, really can feel imaginatively that there is such a thing as trust, that fixedness of it? But I can't ever see it, at least, not in real life. Maybe I've dreamed about it? I'm not sure. Maybe I haven't, probably not. I don't think so. There are lots of worlds in my dreams, but not one of them ever contained trust. And so I think that is why, that must be why I so enjoy conversations with you, Justine. I think a lot of people might find you scary, because there is so much at risk, so much at stake for you, and not even because you really mean it. I imagine you don't mean to risk so much. I feel a kind of responsibility toward you, and not one that I would really have sought out for myself, given the choice. But somehow we've just come to start meeting in this way, haven't we? I remember when I saw you, that time we met, how terrifying that was. You really told me everything. And I don't want to say that you shouldn't trust in that way, because it should be beautiful, it could—"

The artist trails off. The light advising us as to the advisedness of crossing the street has transitioned between foreboding and denial, denial and continuous permission, perhaps ten times during the course of her speech. My face is tight. Probably I want to pee, but I have to make sure that she is done.

I have to let the artist who does x continue speaking because this is what she expects. She expects not only to say these things, but to have them absorbed as tidings of great value, which in some universe they probably are, since what she means is that I clearly do not know how to act. And never will.

I calmly thank the artist. I begin to bid her farewell.

Anyway, she is right. I recall how an acquaintance, another toady of the gallery system, was recently sitting with me in an overpriced vegan deli, talking about how people don't care about the artist who does x's work.

"She's obsessed with how uninterested people are in her

work," the toady was insisting. Then the toady was describing her own impending marriage to another toady also employed by the gallery system. They were plotting their escape. They would move to the countryside and start a nonprofit and cease to be toadies (except, of course, in memory). They would be moving shortly after the wedding, which would take place on the country estate of one of the toadies' childless relatives, not a parent.

"She is very, *very* honest about it," the toady was saying, of the artist who does x. "She's just like everyone else, except she's so totally honest. It's amazing you can make a career out of that."

It is true, I think, the artist who does x is honest.

And, as we are kissing the air in front of each other's faces on the corner of 18th Street, I recall another meeting with the artist who does x, one that took place a year earlier, one which the artist herself clearly has not forgotten. During the course of this meeting, the artist who does x acknowledged that she was aware that I was in the midst of becoming divorced from someone I had married when I was in my early twenties, a thing not really done in these parts—the child marriage, I mean.

We were in a bar and restaurant, farther downtown. The artist who does x was comfortably ensconced on an upholstered item. I knew her less well, then.

"He wasn't," I remember telling her, "very nice to me." I meant my former husband.

It was a euphemism.

I watched changes transpiring on the face of the artist who does x. If I had known the artist who does x better at this time, I would have known that the artist who does x was attempting to gauge the required amount of remorse. I did not know then that she is like a paid griever, a mourner for hire. She will exchange the favor of sadness with you, but you must offer something in return.

Because I am poor and essentially useless to the artist who does x's career, what I had to give in this moment was information.

"He didn't," the artist who does x wanted to know, "*hit* you?"

I remember that time became slushy and dim. I looked at the artist who does x's eyes, which were like two lacquered raisins, merciless and slightly too small for her face. I knew that if I said no, the artist who does x would turn away from me, and that this turning away would be for all time. I knew that the artist who does x did not wish to discuss with me the politics of domestic economies, various forms of entitlement. She was not interested in my identity or gender, any more than she was interested in the identity or gender of anyone else. These were mere representations, and representations were not her concern.

The artist who does x wanted to know what had happened.

And I saw that in this moment she was giving me an out. She was letting me know that if I could demonstrate to her satisfaction that my current lamentable status in the world was not a predicament of my own devising, she would be willing to withhold at least 15 percent of the judgment she was otherwise planning to level in my direction.

Oh, how I wanted that 15 percent mercy. And oh how I wanted her to share a bit of sadness with me.

So I paid.

The Poisoners

There once was a man in his thirties. In fact, he seemed younger than this. He lived in the United States of America, which was a country he preferred not to leave, if at all possible. He was married, and he and his wife rented a medium-size apartment in a major city. They paid somewhat less for their apartment than it was customary to pay because the apartment was out of the way, in an inconvenient if OK neighborhood. They had no children and kept no pets. They owned a car but had no savings.

The man, whose name was Will, worked at a framer's, and Will framed prints. Will's wife, whose name was Ada, worked as a freelance fact-checker for magazines. They had fallen deeply in love, years before, in school. Every weekday morning Will rode his bicycle to the framer's, where he had learned to mat and frame and where he now made an increasingly steady living. Ada stayed at the apartment and made use of the Internet.

Will was good at his work at the framer's. His job was not difficult, and he was proud of what he did. Another person might have chafed at the required tasks: collecting measurements, pointing to a wall of samples. Will celebrated his ability to remain alert.

Will remembered that when he was very young he had often been unable to control himself and had done many stupid things. Also, in childhood there were experiences of great beauty. Will waited patiently for the life that was to come.

The framing business, as things turned out, prospered. The owner of the business, a septuagenarian refugee of ethnic cleansing and a late adopter of capitalism, hired a second assistant. The second assistant was a woman. Her name was Jamie. She was small, and she was exactly six months younger than Will. She had grown up on a farm on the other side of the country and possessed an earnest manner.

Jamie, like Will, was married. It was a joke and also a fact: Jamie was married to a man named Jaime. Jamie had taken Jaime's last name, and therefore they were, at least on paper, all but identical.

Jamie and Will joked around at the framer's. They joked about many things. They laughed about Jamie's name. They got to know each other.

Life at work was good.

But life at home was not good for Will.

Could Will have spoken words aloud to tell another person what was wrong? It is certain that he could not; otherwise I wouldn't be telling this story. No, for Will, as far as his wife, Ada, was concerned, there were no words to describe what was wrong. Ada worked industriously all day. I almost typed "industrially." Yes, she worked hard. And she was successful and began to demand high hourly rates.

This was what everyone knew of Ada and Will: they worked hard and did well in their small jobs and were beloved by those who knew them. They were, to their friends, what is termed a "good couple."

Ada and Will remembered the days when they had fallen in love. Those were the days when they were young. And they were still sort of young, but increasingly less so. And Ada kept house, but she did not like to cook because cooking dirtied the kitchen. In fact, Will found the house *too* clean. He often wished he had something to eat.

During this time, Ada and Will were becoming, unknowingly, exactly what they believed themselves not to be. This point is very important. (If you are reading this in a print format, it is suggested you highlight or underline this paragraph. If web, it is suggested you copy and paste the text into a browser plug-in, or other, for future reference. If you are reading this story for a class, please do not email me about it. I feel uncomfortable when I get these sorts of messages and don't know what to do. I figure, however, that I may, without veering into the territory of unfair assistance, alert you here that something significant has come up. You'll want to use your independent powers of deduction to figure out what it means.) And so:

At work, Will and Jamie joked a lot. Jamie told Will about the food she ate. She fed him easily, carelessly, from Tupperware she brought to the framer's from her home. One of the things Jamie frequently did at home was to cook.

Will ceased wishing that he had something to eat. He ate the food Jamie brought to him. He was kinder to Ada. Briefly, he felt satisfied. Will and Jamie went out to drinks after work.

Ada, meanwhile, stopped freelancing and got an office job and was promoted. She, perhaps, was satisfied, too.

Ada gave a great deal to her job. Perhaps, indistinctly, to her it meant freedom. The job made others aware of her existence. She used some of the money she made to purchase a more expensive phone.

She sometimes, perhaps often, returned home late, after 9:00 p.m. She went to professional parties. She sometimes returned home after three o'clock in the morning.

Ada, Ada, blah, blah, blah. Other people, at the place where Ada worked and at other adjacent places, were interested in Ada. Ada this, Ada that. "Ada," they said, "it's you!" They said, "Your name is a palindrome, how funny!" They were hard to ignore, even in their senseless interest. They were interested, too, that Ada was so young yet had been married for so long. Ada attempted to smile with a certain mystery when she was asked about being a very young married person, who had for so long been married. "Sometimes you just meet the right person," I believe she said, cultivating a kind of haze.

Will, meanwhile, was miserable but savvy. He stayed out late with Jamie, who had been married to Jaime at an even younger age than Will had been married to Ada. There was no question, between them, which is to say, between Will and Jamie, two colleagues at a framer's, of the worth and normalcy of marriage, even in this city—where so many people had been married and divorced, or refused to marry at all.

In the day, the sunlight sifted attractively through the barred windows of the former knitting factory in which the framer's business was located. Dust sparkled. It seemed to carry a promise of truth. It was pure and relevant.

Jamie told Will the story of how Jaime's real first name wasn't really "Jaime." It was Ted. He had changed his name to "Jaime" in marriage.

"Legally?" Will asked.

"Definitely." Jamie laughed.

Will contemplated her word. Perhaps he saw something there, I don't know.

It's hard to tell this story without feeling that every person included in it is incredibly, painfully simple. And yet, these are their real thoughts and actions, insofar as it is given to me to know them. Please don't get on my case about it. These aren't real people, and yet these really are the things they really say and think and do. All these things did happen somewhere. Amazingly, miraculously, the people to whom the things did happen barely thought about the things.

And do I even have to spell it out? Will and Jamie have fallen in love.

Here, a strange thing occurs, because there is a lot that you don't know about Will. Allow me to explain:

Will was, of course, a kind of artist. He just didn't know what kind. He believed that he did not know what kind of artist he was *yet*, but things were more complicated since they were not entirely narrative, in his mind.

Will might never know what kind of artist he was. This was something he allowed himself. He told himself that he was an artist, even if he never managed to make anything. He was an artist, he told himself, of life.

Still, Will was working on it. Will was living. He was constructing something.

The framer's business was located in a rapidly gentrifying industrial area.

The other thing to know about Jamie was that her partner was not well. Jaime was ill. He suffered from a condition doctors had given up trying to diagnose. He was told to maintain a restful lifestyle. He had a temperamental heart. Or maybe it was an autoimmune disorder. I don't mean to seem callous; I'm just not sure.

Anyway, Jamie cooked for Jaime. And there were many plants in their apartment. And Jamie cooked so much for

Jaime that there was often extra food. And now when she came to work she brought with her two lunches, one for herself and one for Will.

It was easy to hide this from Jaime, who never went into the kitchen and busied himself with his record collection most of the time, whenever he was not lying down.

Ada did not feed Will. In fact, all pretense of cooking had ceased with her. She purchased meals at overpriced locations near her office. And sometimes she did not eat at all. Thinness was valued in her industry.

Jamie told Will that she wished that Jaime were not sick. It was unfair, she knew, but she could not help feeling that his refusal to become well reflected poorly on her efforts. Jaime meanwhile did go to work and did know other people. His was not the life of an invalid.

And yet, said Jamie (if not in quite so many words), I heal him just enough that he maintains some modicum of independence. I do not heal him enough that he becomes truly well. I cannot heal him into a state of equity with me; I cannot create in him an equal partner.

I have, Jamie said, known Ted for too long.

Will was not sure what Jamie was trying to say.

Will was generally uncertain.

And now Ada traveled for work. She left for three or four days at a time. She did not think very much about her marriage. Ada was working.

So this is a pretty good summary of the lives and probable

sentiments of these two women. Will was somebody who knew them both. He knew them both and felt a great number of powerful things where both of them were concerned! It's so hard to say, at this moment, what exactly was happening!

And now at work, Will and Jamie ate. They sat down to lunch together. From her bag, Jamie brought forth small bluish containers. In the containers were carefully composed salads including grains and proteins. There was a set of four mini-scones baked without the use of dairy products. There was a vegan pudding and a lentil-based pasta dish.

They ate at first in silence. Elsewhere at the framer's, others did not yet break for lunch. Still other workers were relatives of the owner.

Will and Jamie observed these people where they moved.

Will and Jamie had lived through numerous points in time and each had grown up in a family, but they felt unprepared for what was occurring at this moment.

The world was attempting to recompose itself. It was no longer a scene. Now it had grown soft. It was a blanket. It rushed toward them, plush and ready to conform.

They were observing a slowly coalescing geometric shape.

Will and Jamie could barely look at each other.

Will took out one of his notebooks. *Hey there Pony*, he wrote at the top of a blank page.

Hi, wrote Jamie, circling the word. She must have been able to feel her heart floating in her neck like a pickled cherry.

No one around Will and Jamie knew anything about

what they said. They spoke without speaking and the world, the phenomenal world and time and chance, permitted this to happen. Nothing stood in their way. This was how they knew that they were doing the right thing.

In their writing, Jamie and Will recognized something. What they recognized was not a thing that could, per se, be seen. It was a feeling, and it was impersonal. It was a knowing that you had to choose.

Just as, before a line was drawn in black ballpoint on a page, there was no line; just as, at first there was nothing and later something did occur and in this event things were no longer the same; just so, Jamie and Will perceived that they no longer inhabited the worlds they had inhabited when first they met. They inhabited a single world, and it was new.

They were very, very much in love.

On the one hand, this was for them a beautiful and graceful thing. On the other, this meant that they had broken promises once central to their lives. And it was for this reason, the "other hand," that they for many months did nothing.

They did nothing, that is, except that they began to make love. I'm saying, they had coitus, and really quite a lot of it, which they in turn documented for the usual reasons, using their phones.

On some level, it's hard for anyone to say how it is, precisely, that sex changes things. It's fun, and it reminds us that someday we will die, and it can make us inclined to feel more tenderly toward a given person—and, perhaps, more and more inclined to return to that person's physical proximity.

Will and Jamie noticed what was beginning to occur. They wanted to be together all the time. For this reason, they decided to perform an experiment.

Will and Jamie resolved that they would spend more time alone together, as well as more time together with their spouses, alone. And they would also cause their spouses to meet, and all four of them would spend more time together.

It was an experiment. It was an experiment to see if Will and Jamie could understand their feelings for each other. Maybe these feelings, while strong, didn't matter and weren't significant. If so, they needed to know.

Will and Jamie were good people. They were people who were willing to find out if what they were doing was not good and therefore wrong. They were decent, thoughtful people and you could not fault them for not being thorough. They were performing an experiment so that they could be sure. They were hardworking. They wanted what was best.

And so Will and Jamie and Ada and Jaime, or, rather, Will and Ada and Jaime and Jamie, went out to a bar. It was a bar in a relatively remote part of the city, and it was also a bar Will and Jamie had visited together. Ada drove the four of them, in the car she owned with Will.

They all drank several beers together. They talked about the city and the choice all four had made to move to it. It was a choice that defined their lives and it was something they had in common.

For Ada and Jaime, this was an unremarkable night. They were with their spouses and spoke with their spouses' unremarkable coworkers. Ada did not find Jaime, or Jamie, for that matter, particularly interesting. Jaime thought Ada was cagey, if tall. Who knows what Jaime thought of Will. Will and Jamie silently loved each other and did not let on. They did not so much as permit their eyes to meet. You could see this as a kind of comedy of errors, but in fact matters had already swerved a rather fateful swerve. Will and Jamie watched as their partners blindly took part. For it was far, far easier to do all this than they had imagined. Ada and Jaime trusted Will and Jamie. Ada and Jaime lived in the past. Only Will and Jamie knew this. Only Will and Jamie had managed to move on, to enter the present. God bless America.

But it wasn't really so simple. Will and Jamie could not go directly on to triumph in their love and shared sense of justice, because Jaime was always slightly ill, and this summoned Jamie back to him. He needed someone to offer him soups and compresses, to listen to his complaints. Jamie went to him freely. Jamie didn't seem to mind.

Jamie sometimes left work directly, in order to tend to Jaime.

Jamie is a saint, thought Will. She understands need. She does not ignore the real, true need of others. She is a good person in this uneven world and an authentic person, and this is why I love her.

Ada was not a good person. She wasn't a bad person, either. She was just neutral. She wasn't authentic. She went to her job.

On some level, Ada must have understood this about herself. Everything she did now appeared to be about working. Everything in the world appeared to feel so neutral to her.

Will wondered how he could love someone so beset by neutrality.

Will saw that without Jamie, he was completely alone.

By this time a year had passed. It was even more than a year. No, by now two years had passed, and Will and Jamie had spent a great deal of time alone, together with their spouses, and with their spouses, together. They had also spent a great deal of time together, alone. They were also in possession of an extensive photographic archive of their love.

In some ways, it was a functional arrangement. Yet, both Will and Jamie had to wonder, was (*is*) it possible to live without lies?

They each, separately, thumbed through their digital images. They sent old images to each other, growing nostalgic, growing aroused. Things entered other things. Stuff was offered, held. They even created new images, in their joy. They wanted to be free.

It was for this reason, this desire on their part to learn if it might be possible to live without lying, that Will and

Jamie decided to make a change. Believe me, by the way, that their confidants on both sides warned against it. Will and Jamie had told some people what was going on, of course, and those people, the aware people, the trusted ones, were warning them against this step. These people were warning them because these people saw that the current arrangement was a livable one. These people were realists. Some of them were even married. Don't fix what isn't broken, these sage people said, usually employing profanity.

It might seem remarkable that anyone would consider Will and Jamie's situation a happy compromise, but there were actual people living on the planet who felt this way. Perhaps it says something about the sort of people Will and Jamie chose as friends, I don't really know.

However, I should note that this was not enough for Will and Jamie. Will and Jamie didn't care what their most trusted, wisest friends told them regarding balance and being happy with the life one has. They both wanted to know what would happen if they were to stop lying.

The other thing is, both Will and Jamie were also of the mind that they never wanted to stop lying, ever. And it was the fact that telling the truth, so called, was incompatible with never ever stopping lying, that tripped them up. It felt fresh to them and new, the idea of ceasing to conceal themselves. They wanted that piquant as-yet-un-experienced experience. They didn't want to stop lying, but they were also greedy for new life and refused to be denied. They looked at each other and told each other that there existed an experience that should be tried, a sort of paradise, whee!

They were for a long time baffled as to how to do it. For, as time had gone on, as we have noted, the situation had become increasingly settled and tenable. It also felt right to leave things as they were. This was why Will and Jamie resorted to occult measures.

I know, said Jamie, a sort of spell by means of which we can allow chance to make our difficult decision for us. She didn't, by the way, say this in so many words.

Will looked at Jamie. She was a brunette, with spindly limbs.

Just leave your phone out where Ada can find it, Jamie said.

Will understood what Jamie was saying without so many words. He understood that he and Jamie could allow others to make their decision for them. It would be possible to demonstrate that the reason he and Jamie were lying was not that he and Jamie were liars but that they were doing something that others were not willing to perceive, given the terrifying truth of his and Jamie's feelings for each other.

And so, because of the ultimate hiddenness of truth, because truth loves to hide, as the ancient philosophers mutter damply into their beards, Will did as Jamie suggested. He left his smartphone lying around and he put a very obvious security code on it, one that even an extremely inauthentic individual would be able to guess. And he and Jamie waited for several months.

It took longer than they expected for Ada to consult the phone. The results of this consultation were predictable and we needn't linger on them. Of greater interest is what was simultaneously occurring in the world of Jamie and Jaime, because actually very little was occurring there.

Will now lived alone. He had left the apartment he shared with Ada and moved to an even more remote part of the city. Here, the ocean exchanged colors with the sky.

Meanwhile, Jamie and Jaime lived together. Will and Jamie saw each other but they did not speak of Jaime. In truth, they did not really see each other much.

Will did not feel fear. Will felt only a calm confusion that approached a form of devastation or collapse. Again, Will was calm. He was calm as someone in the midst of a calamity is calm. Will waited. And he waited some more.

Will had done nothing. He had only done as Jamie had said.

All contact between Will and Ada had ceased. Will knew this was a permanent state of affairs.

Will went for walks by the ocean. He drank. He felt himself changing.

Will received a contract regarding his separation from Ada as well as information about their impending divorce. Later, Will received papers regarding the divorce.

Will signed these papers.

Meanwhile, Jamie was distant. Even without asking her about it, Will knew that Jaime, her husband, was sick.

On the day on which the divorce came through, a strange thing happened: Jaime died. I guess Ted died, too. His heart stopped, or there was some other systemic failure.

The upscale grocery store where Jaime/Ted worked posted a notice online and in its newsletter. Relatives paid for a few sentences in a major newspaper.

Will did not know what Jaime/Ted knew about Will's relationship with Jamie, and now Will would never know.

I don't know what Jaime/Ted knew, either.

Eleven months later, Will and Jamie got married and moved out of the city. They were finally going to start their new life. This is the sort of thing, in case you were wondering, that is possible.

More months have gone by and now, in the present, Jamie is pregnant. She stands by a window in the country in the home she shares with Will. This is really occurring, by the way. Dust spots the sunbeams and leaves rustle. It seems like there is always good light around these people! Songbirds are singing their hearts out.

Jamie says, "I always knew that I would have to leave Ted."

She calls him Ted these days. It turns out that perhaps this was the name she had always called him, after all.

"I know you knew," says Will. He is interacting with a dog.

"It became clearer and clearer," Jamie continues. "I

wanted him to go away. It's not like it is with you. I wanted him to leave me."

"I guess, in a sense, he did." Will is solemn.

"You're not listening to me. He shouldn't have let me make so much food for him. He knew I grew up on a farm. Everyone knew."

Will continues to stroke the face of his dog. Jamie is speaking but Will lets the words she says accumulate at a distance. The words take the form of soft, dark clumps. Will thinks about the brave dominion of man, the chaos of animal life in the absence of a master.

Will thinks.

Will begins thinking about what Jamie has said, moments ago. It never occurred to him until this minute that Jamie could have left Ted, but she could have. Yes! She could have left him early on, years ago, at the very beginning. She could have left him even before Will knew her.

But Ted is dead, thinks Will. No one has to leave a dead man.

Will begins to listen.

Jamie is saying, "He wasn't strong enough. But now that I am feeding two people again, I can feel how I understand humanity better. It's so important, what I learned."

"You did the right thing," Will reassures her meaninglessly. Will's dog stares at him with melted eyes. "You knew what was the right thing to do. You always do."

Will says these things and thinks he understands what Jamie says. He thinks that Jamie is saying that one must have standards. One cannot judge a bond, even of love, without a test. One is right to be suspicious, especially if one cannot understand a partner's behavior. He is glad that he and his new wife are so well matched. He is glad they will bring life into the world.

Guy

This article is about the persons. For other uses, see <u>Guy</u> (disambiguation).

Guy is an American <u>slang</u> term for a human being.[1] It characteristically applies to <u>men</u>.

Guy is an old term, recognized by multiple generations.[2]

Contents[hide]

1

History

1.1

Guys in literature

1.2

Spread on social media

1.3

Debunking

2

Biography

2.1

Public opinion

3

See also

4

References

5

External links

History[edit]

The term is present in early nineteenth-century <u>British</u> English to indicate a "poorly dressed fellow," originally referring to the effigy of <u>Guy Fawkes</u>, leader of the 1605 <u>Gunpowder Plot</u> to blow up the king and <u>Parliament</u>.[3] It was also a vogue word during the <u>Napoleonic Wars</u>. However, it is commonly believed that there were no true guys until the <u>1970s</u>.[4][5] There is thought to be a link between the development of the term into a social phenomenon and the financialization of <u>oil</u> markets and <u>stagflation</u> prevalent in that decade.[6][7][8][9]

In the summer of 1969, during the course of a lecture on social ecology under late <u>capitalism</u>, the systems theorist <u>Niklas Luhmann</u> noted that the concepts of "generalness" and "individuality" are opposed.[10] Luhmann's theory was shortly tested during the rise to prominence within the American Republican political party of former actor and corporate hype-man, Ronald Reagan, who, although unsuccessful in his 1968 and 1976 bids for the Republican nomination for the presidency, yet embodied the so-called everyman quality definitively described by Alfred Döblin in his 1929 novel, *Berlin Alexanderplatz*, even as Regan vociferously touted the uniqueness and irreplaceability of America.[11][12][13]

After Reagan was elected to the presidency in 1980 by a nearly 10% margin, Luhmann's theory of Western social systems was at last disproved.[14] In urban America, the term "guy" came into frequent use, usually deployed to address someone in an informal manner ("So listen, guy, I'm glad you finally called") or refer to another person ("Well, wouldn't you know, that guy's stealing my car"). Use of the word to mean "person" was further popularized in American films of the 1980s and 1990s such as *Teenage Mutant Ninja Turtles*, *The Truth About Cats & Dogs*, and *Titanic*. Infamously, the unreleased director's cut of *Titanic* contains an anachronistic use of the term, when actor Billy Zane, playing the role of Cal Hockley originally written for Michael Douglas, points at a lifeboat and begins screaming uncontrollably about his irrational fear of flowering plants. This scene was deleted for the theatrical version.[15][16]

The late 1990s saw the solidification of guys, leading to the period of the early aughts sometimes referred to as "peak guyness." The particular inoffensiveness and gangsterism, typified by the ubiquity of <u>drab</u> garments like the <u>cargo short</u>, <u>cargo pant</u>, semi-mesh <u>cargo-T</u>, and <u>golf</u> visor, seemed to come at the expense of political will and directedness, not to mention <u>mental health</u>, for adherents.[17][18] Into the American imagination came an obsession with plots and a prurient interest in that which is unique but, <u>paradoxically</u>, assimilable to even the most unsubtle <u>norms</u>. <u>Authenticity</u> became a frequent theme of American broadcast television, with the ascent of *celebutante* <u>Paris Hilton</u> as well as, later, satirist <u>Stephen Colbert</u>, both of whom played strategically tweaked approximations of themselves.[*citation needed*]

However, since approximately 2008, it has become more common for people to believe that guys do not exist, that there are only <u>men</u>. In fact, studies have shown that guyness is even more prevalent and may not be related to <u>biological</u> <u>sex</u>.[19] Researchers who once mistakenly linked guyness to <u>uncertainty</u> about masculine <u>roles</u> in an increasingly automated society now see the trend as the result of unconscious, as well as conscious, assumption of economic privilege in <u>youth</u>. Guyness has also been shown to lead to alterations in everyday speech patterns among subjects monitored. Meanwhile, <u>Katy Perry</u> is <u>almost</u> certainly a member of the Illuminati.[20][21][22][23]

Guys in literature[edit]

According to the writer <u>Tom Wolfe</u>, no guys have ever appeared in <u>literature</u>.[24] There is, however, some suspicion that the character <u>Jessica Fletcher</u>, portrayed for many years by actress <u>Angela Lansbury</u> on the long-running television series *Murder, She Wrote*, was an attempt to represent a guy as an omnipotent literary mystery writer, under the guise of a female <u>persona</u>.[*citation needed*] As everyone says, there couldn't have been so many murders in one town! The website pentropy.com, citing a <u>4chan</u> post from August 18, 2007, claims that <u>novelist</u> <u>Jonathan Franzen</u> always inserts a small, distant figure into the forest scenes in his novels. The figure climbs a difficult-to-perceive <u>ladder</u> and several moments later it is possible to make out the figure swinging back and forth, as if at the end of a hangman's noose. This strange, seemingly unmotivated <u>event</u> is believed by a small cohort of readers, as the cohort's self-proclaimed leader "r3dord3d" notoriously posted, to represent a figure of <u>mourning</u> for the death of guys within <u>art</u>.[25][26] Similarly, <u>Italo Calvino</u>'s ghost is said to wander the rambles of Prospect Park, manifesting himself in picnickers' speech through uncanny bursts of whimsy. It's embarrassing for me to say how <u>I</u> came to this conclusion, but I know he's there.[27]

Spread on social media[edit]

Aaron Rally-Wyeth, a New York writer and editor, was dubbed "a guy" by Facebook users reacting to his post of August 18, 2016, in which he compared "hair plugs" to "butt plugs" for, as he wrote in a follow-up post, "no particular reason," appending a PDF of over 1,000 images of the Canadian-American actor Brendan Fraser. "Who is this guy?" wrote one Facebook commenter, Pika Shoe. "I feel like, yeah."[28] In response, Rally-Wyeth commented with a link to a tweet by Justin Bieber, in which Bieber expressed a desire to distance himself from his own father. This statement, since removed from the original post, subsequently became the basis of a theory of the interrelation of male passivity and apocalyptic dread, popularly known as "Whose Guy Theory," or, colloquially, "wgt." It appeared on Twitter via a since-deleted account attributed to "Brüno Mars." The theory was then posted to the message board Godlike Productions. Rally-Wyeth denied that he had any intent to "even know anything about your dad."[29] This phrase later became a rallying cry for Fraser's fans, who, long silent, began to demand that a prequel to 1999's colonial Pandora's box retelling, *The Mummy*, be made in which Fraser's character Rick O'Connell's relationship with his apparently kind and successful, although in fact conniving and acquisitive, father is revealed to have been the driving animus behind O'Connell's obsession with the looting of ancient Egyptian graves. Actor Rachel Weisz is said to be in talks to produce.[30]

Debunking [edit]

All this was subsequently shown not to matter. No one was looking, but it was obvious, all the same. There in the dregs of various parties, in the calm and bitter talk that succeeds a success, in the desperate mashing of the foggy and barely responsive screen of an iPhone 5. Unseasonable weather was the first topic broached; after this, all could agree. Culture was something anyone "had." It was influenced; it got produced. That guy had a knowing way of walking into anyone's scenario. I met him through some acquaintances.[by whom?]

Biography[edit]

Born in West Suburb, Connecticut, Rally-Wyeth attended the Trask-Lovely School and the University of Chicago, where he majored in the History of Social Thought. After graduating, Rally-Wyeth relocated to Berlin, Germany, where he held various positions, as a teacher of English as well as what he termed a "technological advisor to naïve gallerists" in his well-known humor piece, "Late Imperialism: Or, While the Soft Power Lasts."[31] In 2007 he returned to New York City, settling in the Prospect Heights neighborhood of Brooklyn, a rapidly gentrifying area where all his friends were moving.[32]

Rally-Wyeth rose to prominence with a series of unpaid internships at general interest publications where, by going out to drinks with senior staff and <u>googling</u> them beforehand, he established himself as an <u>unshy</u> <u>heterosexual</u> individual of note. By early 2008, he had risen to the position of "Janitor," the waggishly titled part-time role on the masthead of *Man's Leisure*, a magazine which has since been sold, restructured, and rebranded as the print quarterly of <u>*Buzzfeed*</u>, <u>*Print*</u>.[33] Though Rally-Wyeth's tenure as Janitor lasted but a short year, he was able to revitalize *Man's Leisure*'s standing among the younger intelligentsia of Brooklyn, frequently leaning ironically in to what he and colleagues called the "badness" of the journal's name. In 2009, he was the subject of a major advertising campaign for <u>That Most Important Thing</u>, the lifestyle brand and for-profit philanthropy group, which was then honing in on "the muted palette of male fashion" and developing a line of small luggage for discerning younger urbanites, what later became the cult "<u>Petit-Maître</u>" <u>murse</u> series, with the slogan "For a Living Religion."[34]

Meanwhile, Rally-Wyeth continued to post to social media. In 2011, he went public with his boutique media company, <u>TK</u>, so named for the editorial convention indicating text to be inserted at a later time. TK's early mission was to "publish" <u>tote bags</u> at irregular intervals, as the firm wrote in its <u>print-on-demand</u> manifesto, "<u>Successfully Marketed Lives</u>." Of this endeavor, Rally-Wyeth posted:

> And now, for all this perennial Martyrdom,
> and Poesy, and even Prophecy, what is it
> that this Guy asks in return? Solely, I may
> say, that you would recognize his existence;
> would admit him to be a living object; or,
> even failing this, a visual object, or thing
> that will reflect rays of light . . .[35]

After an initial backlash, Rally-Wyeth published a retraction and personal statement in which he admitted that there were other people participating in his collective and his use of the first-person singular pronoun was disingenuous. He also admitted that he had appropriated all the text in his social media updates from real-estate listings and homeopathic tea packaging. TK subsequently initiated efforts to diversify its staff. The rarity of people actually from New York City within New York City became a point of controversy in nearby milieus, culminating in Rally-Wyeth's viral think piece, "'Where Did *I* Grow Up?'?"[36]

Since 2016, Rally-Wyeth has taken on an advisory role within TK in order to focus on his web series, "Spreading 2.0." He divides his time between Brooklyn and various grant-funded opportunities, with his partner and .63 children.[37]

Public opinion[edit]

The world was changing. I lived in it, but if you had blinked, you might have missed me. I stood in the shadows, the corridor, the edge of all things, and I was vaguely this guy's friend. I had at least the same level of education as him, if not more, and my face was reasonably <u>symmetrical</u>. I had less hair on my <u>body</u>, although my body was larger than his. When we first met, things were professional and, indeed, have basically remained so.[eh?]

But it's more complicated than I am letting on. I began working with him not just because I believed in his economic-miracle-cum-personal-brand (that everyone kept photographing and re-blogging and ostentatiously letting slip whenever it took the form of a name), but because I was an idealist who had difficulty holding on to a job. I may have needed someone to help me. I might have wanted to get involved with the free market. I encountered this guy's friends at informal gatherings and they told me how good he was with money. Of course, they used different terms. They didn't say "cash" or "aggressive" or "demonically clever" or "red-blooded systems juggernaut." It was more like that party game where you have to guess a word without being supplied any of its common synonyms. It was maybe like <u>Charades</u>, too, but I think that came later. Only later was it necessary to attempt to interpret events without listening to anything

you heard. Only later did I get to be in an <u>Odysseus</u>-type situation, in which the majority-minority ratio on the ship was
inverted and I was the only one with wax in her ears.[38] No,
in the beginning it was more like, "We have to get in front
of this moment and this is the way to do it. These assorted
institutions are failing and everyone is out of touch. You ar-
en't recognized because you haven't found the right partners.
Our bubble is the best bubble that ever bubbled, ever, OK?"
And I believed it. I believed them. I believed everything I
heard. I believed I was being rescued from the world's larg-
est and most inexorably creeping (due to carbon emissions)
desert.

Maybe it was even true. Maybe I was airlifted out. I stopped
freelancing and obtained healthcare. My groceries went <u>or-
ganic</u>. It's the same old story of the same old success in the
same old floating world, or <u>*ukiyo*</u> (浮世), which, if you're interested, is another name for urban lifestyle in <u>Edo-era</u> Japan
(1603–1868), a time of bewildering quantities of <u>sumptuary
laws</u>. In the/a floating world, elaborate forms of luxury come
into existence because it is necessary that landless persons
have something low-key to spend their money on. I mean,
here I'm just talking about housing being prohibitively expensive, which is not exactly the same thing as legally orga-
nized restriction, but some of the effects are similar. I was
also working a lot in that guy's company, which gave me almost no time. I needed the new money I earned to pay for

new services I was no longer able to use my own uncompen-
sated labor to obtain. Here I am talking about cashew-violet-
kale smoothies, for example, and laundry. But it went beyond
this. When I rode the subway, which was every day I didn't
take a car due to exhaustion brought on by constant access to
email, I carried a little notebook, and in this little notebook I
recorded the enviable qualities of other people's shoes. Using
this information, I later scoured the Internet. I got really into
it. I had whole outfits. I had zero friends but got plenty of joy
from <u>mimesis</u>. My posts did pretty well. To the outside world
I appeared bright and fluid and ageless.[39]

In reality, the company, a.k.a. TK Industries, LLC, hence-
forth, TK, had an open-plan office. If for some reason you
do not already know, these are the worst. Everyone is sur-
veilling everyone, it's not just a powerful-on-weak sort of
situation. You'd think that at the end of the day this would
make things more democratic, nonhierarchical, and so on,
but the outcome is actually ambient <u>terror</u>. And the wages
of ambient terror in business relations are: elastic factions,
pointless miniature power grabs, bursts of autocratic rule,
ugh. By far the worst of it was we knew so much about him,
our guy, Andrew, a.k.a. Andy, a.k.a. A. We knew when he
started sleeping with the twenty-three-year-old who was
helping out during tax season, and we watched as she was
kept on beyond her initial contract, and we were mesmerized
as it continued and slowly but surely she began to lose her

mind. Now the twenty-three-year-old floated into the office. She was a mannequin dangling from the ceiling by a wire. "Oh *God*," said someone, once it was assumed she was out of earshot. On the subway home we'd all attempt to talk it out. We were still pretty sure we were doing something revolutionary at TK and, pursuant to this, that A. and his partner must have an <u>open relationship</u>. People went to great lengths to explain it to themselves. A.'s partner, a widely admired immigration lawyer, had to know and had to be OK with it. If the twenty-three-year-old was in such bad shape, it had to be the twenty-three-year-old's fault, issues with her dad and so on, because everyone else's behavior was definitely aboveboard. Or maybe we didn't try that hard to convince ourselves. I'm not exactly sure what we said. Maybe we said nothing. Maybe we talked about how thrilling all our opportunities at TK were and how we ought to try our darndest not to fuck this astonishing life-work situation up. The twenty-four-hour access kitchen contained: a lifetime supply of "naturally" flavored <u>Perrier</u>, leaky espresso machine donated by somebody's parents, miscellaneous takeout cutlery, plus endless packets of SUGAR IN THE RAW and early-industrial <u>silverfish</u> civilization.[40]

I'd go to lunch with A. He was actually kind of a <u>weirdo</u>, with gentle, immature leanings, and I liked him for this. I enjoyed the references to his suburban childhood and the obscure collecting practices that had made him into the relentlessly successful autodidact that he was. I thought: *It's nice not to be lost in the desert.* I was now on a road to the new <u>New Arcadia</u>, and A. was my compass.[41] A. was also the road, the wheels on my <u>low-emission vehicle</u>; he was the lush encampment, its verdant bower, the most enlightened thought leader known to man, and here I was at his feet, a clean animal free of disease. Did I dream of killing him, sometimes? Did I aspire to sip his warm blood from a pliable SOLO cup? Num num. It would be pointless to pretend that I did not. This, as everyone knows, is the nature of the civilizing impulse; you understand that someone has to die for any new politics to be born. You just have to have the stomach for it. You should additionally bear in mind that, if successful, you may be next.

I was not the murdering kind, as it turned out, but I did have something of a death wish. I also was very interested in other people's blind spots: it's this altruistic part of me that's meanwhile sort of evil. It might have something to do with problems in my own family. A. and I were eating lunch all the time and I was all the time talking to my colleagues at TK on the subway. Slowly but surely, inexorably even, I came to see that there was somebody at TK who did not know. By this I mean, there was somebody who did not know what A. and the twenty-three-year-old were getting up to in the backs of taxicabs and in karaoke hall bathrooms and in the office's emergency stairwell and the like, that telltale raspberry flush she wore, his candied, whiskered smirk. This unknowing person

was an advocate of the twenty-three-year-old and this unknowing person was also the second-most-powerful person
at TK. Let us call him B. B. was (1) extremely ambitious and
(2) very clever, but (3) self-effacing to the point of practical
self-annihilation, and what this combination made him was
(4) certifiably insane. There was a part of B. that was capable
of laughing long and hard and even (5) semi-orgasmically at
other people's grief, although he never flushed, ever. All of
the above I found sympathetic and adorable, = on my part,
an enormous error. It was also proof of how deeply involved I
had become with TK, which was increasingly resembling an
American family, along with the predictable heteronorma-
tive drama, rolling of eyes, gnashing of teeth, constant de-
ployment of irony to circumvent honest, useful conversation.
I guess you could say my tastes were changing. B., I thought,
is wonderful.

B. did not take the subway. This fact alone suggests that I
should have had to specially seek him out in order to make
the revelation I was so hell-bent on making. But the thing
is, I didn't. I didn't even have to try! Space and time were,
as it turned out, curved in this org, and for this reason, our
occult relativity, B. blithely came to me. I'm not trying to say
that B. was a good person, by the way. He wasn't. Neither
was A. Neither was I, or, "I.," as I could call myself, a true
"company man." What I'm trying to say is, people can begin
to care for one another in the strangest of fashions. I have

heard that the distinction between geometry and physics is: theoretical versus actual infinity—and subsequent events may have had to do with a category mistake like that. They also had something to do with everyone at TK using language in strange and mesmerizing ways. They always said exactly what they meant, and what they meant was whatever they wanted what they said to mean. A job was "a practice." Money was "a concern." Meanwhile, a lot of allegedly unrelated activity went on.

B. and I. went out of town together one spring. Or, I mean, he and I did. We even drank a glass of wine at a special hilltop location. I was discovering in these moments that I really didn't care too much about my life. I may not have been, ahem, alone in this, but it's still not a particularly pleasant finding. Usually, the way you deal with it is by finally accepting that gift of MDMA at a professional function. B. confined himself to staring at my legs. He was a superb driver. I waited until we were about to return the rental, a tender moment idling on a sagging stretch of BQE, to let him know my suspicions regarding the twenty-three-year-old and A.[42]

Post revelation, B. surprised me by bursting into tears. I mean, he sniffled a little, which, for him, was the equivalent. B. gazed at me—his long-legged colleague—with a mix of hatred, lust, and fear. He must have gone home and vowed revenge and masochistically shoved a random $2K into his IRA, unforced austerity being his sole vice. It was not many weeks before the twenty-three-year-old was mysteriously admitted to a prestigious graduate program in the applied arts and, with calculated lament, diligently let go.

This should have been the end of the story, but sadly it was not. There were a bunch of loose ends, including my prurient interest in others' blind spots and the mingled rage and gratitude B. now felt toward me because I had so casually pointed out his vision troubles in sluggish traffic. There was, B. had come to feel, something about him only I could see. And, although I really didn't know him at all, B. was convinced I had lately joined him at the secret center of his life—a psychic locus analogous to QuickBooks.[citation needed]

I, meanwhile, watched A., who had no idea I—or, *I.*—was the one responsible for his deprivation. There was no doubt about it, anodyne although the event had seemed, the loss of the sweet-faced twenty-three-year-old, along with her fuchsia flushes, was a blow. A. acquired those physical tics popular culture associates with zombies or tame deer fed on Hostess cakes.[43] He began to treat the office like it was his living room. We saw a lot more of his socks and smelled *a lot* more of some sort of gluten-free casserole. Maybe A. hadn't been aware of the strength of his feelings. Subway gossip shifted. Fewer people confessed.

I., meanwhile, if only to avoid the weeping casseroles, began going out to lunch with B. I. and B. had a lot of brilliant ideas together. B. even wanted I. to replace A. I mean, it's getting <u>tragic</u> pretty quickly now. I. can't fathom B.'s desires. B. would like I. to dance continuously on a <u>pedestal</u>. I. should dance as well as is humanly possible. While I. is dancing so admirably well and receiving inhuman quantities of adulation, B. is going to run off at a certain distance and get a very big gun, which he is planning to train on her. It's unlikely that he'll pull the trigger but, hey, this is New York, and, as they say, you never know. Should I. jump, or must she maintain her meticulous shimmy? Turn to page 231 if you choose life. If you don't choose life, what kind of person are you?

By now, you should be able to hear A. chuckling in the background. Once he gets control of himself, you can make out his soft and buoyant words. He's muttering something about how most people never see it coming. For my part, I'm whispering that he's right, A.'s very right, and, by the way, if he's still planning on stopping by my desk at noon, can he please deliver a sack or two of miscellaneous opiates, plus some sort of blood-staunching device? A. isn't the worst guy, after all. He forgave me pretty quickly for having to abruptly quit my job.

Guy

See also^[edit]

But the story does not end here.

A. called me once, recently, now that we are truly adults, or trying to be adults again, while I was out of town on a vacation slash exile, and he wouldn't stop talking about this one thing, about how when he walks by a mirror sometimes it will give no reflection. This seemed like a bizarre cliché to me, vampires etc., and I tried to change the metaphor to one about <u>passivity</u>, but I quickly realized A. wasn't joking. Something had <u>happened</u> since we'd stopped working together, and this something wasn't good. Nervous now, I hastily recommended A. read that very old novel about the Princess de Clèves. I admit it felt like a funny suggestion, since it goes against gender norms and also reminds you of high school French. A guy wouldn't read that book! But I. wanted A. to. More seriously, this might be the only thing that can help A. see who he is becoming.

In <u>*La Princess de Clèves*</u> two people never consummate their passion for each other. I. didn't mention this novel because it has anything to do with the two of us/them in that sense— rather, I. mentioned it because it is a novel that describes what happens when it seems like nothing does. I. wanted A. to see that not all passivity comes at the expense of action.[44]

Anyway, I'm just observing things: the incredible sociability and complexity of this guy's life; my love for him and his strange, macho androgyny, which, in spite of all that I have written above, still seems genuine—the love, I mean, not the <u>machismo</u>.[45] I couldn't save A. and, perplexingly, he couldn't save me, either. So sometimes we're on email. We'll go out for a platonic dinner and I'll permit myself to look at his hands.

References

1. <u>"Are You Ready for Ghosting, Benching and Getting Curved?"</u> <u>*MenHow*</u>. December 28, 2017. Retrieved April 30, 2018.

2. Kushner, Ashton (April 20, 2011). <u>"Working with Five Working Generations of Workers in Today's Competitive Workplace."</u> *Forbes*. Retrieved April 30, 2018.

3. Wall, Stacey (November 4, 2011). <u>"Guy Fawkes's Plot to Make Tony Blair President."</u> *The Telegraph*. Retrieved April 30, 2018.

4. Hookway, Natalie (May 28, 2013). <u>"99 Unbelievable Things American Women Could Not Do Before the 1970s."</u> *Ms. Magazine*. Retrieved April 30, 2018.

5. Truthsman, Leonidas (August 16, 2008). <u>"Pragmatism."</u> *Stanford Encyclopedia of Philosophy*. Retrieved April 30, 2018.

6. Fattouh, Bassam (March 28, 2012). <u>"The Financialization of Oil Markets: Impacts and Evidence."</u> The Oxford Institute for Energy Studies. Retrieved April 30, 2018.

7. Xiong, Wei (2014). <u>"The Financialization of Commodity Markets."</u> <u>*The National Bureau of Economic Research Reporter*</u>. Retrieved April 30, 2018.

8. H. Bestbinder, "Systematic Risk, Hedging Pressure, and Risk

Premiums in Futures Markets," *Review of Financial Studies*, 4 (1992), pp. 637-67; G. Gordo and G. Ochen, "Fantasies about Commodity Futures," *Financial Analysts Journal*, 62 (2) (2006), pp. 47–68; C. Erb and C. Harv, "The Strategic and Tactical Value of Commodity Futures," *Financial Analysts Journal*, 62 (2) (2006), pp. 69–97.

9. Astuces, Sergio (2e semester/Autumn 2008). "Finance-Led Crisis." *Révue de la regulation*. Retrieved April 30, 2018.

10. Lapenn, Santos (April 2009). "Digital Media and Forfeiture of Representative Power." Retrieved April 30, 2018.

11. Uitbundig, Jesse (September 15, 2015). "Bush Fam for the Three-Peat?" *Politico*. Retrieved May 5, 2018.

12. Dollmayor, Bathsheba (1988). *Vagueness in the Berlin Novels of Alfred Döblin*. University of California Press. ISBN 978-3-16-1484.

13. Egileak, Crispin, (2013). "The Soviet Ark as Political Theater." Electronic Theses and Dissertations.

14. *Nineteen Eighty-Four: Science Between Utopia and Dystopia*. Volume 8 of *Sociology of the Sciences Yearbook*. Editors O. Rohrer, H. Well.

15. Volk, Adonis (March 29, 2012). "Film-Bösewicht Billy Zane: Seine Karriere sank mit 'Titanic.'" *Der Spiegel*. Retrieved May 14, 2018.

16. Lewis, Carol. *The Unbeatable, So-Easy-You'll-Pinch-Yourself Self-Hypnosis Cure for Phobia of Flowers (Anthophobia)*. Infiniti Self. eBook.

17. "The Worst Men's Fashion Trends of All Time." (January 31, 2018). *FashionNewbs*. Retrieved May 14, 2018.

18. "Mental Illness Ravages American Economy." (March 1, 2012.) *Scientific American*. Retrieved May 14, 2018.

19. Eckt, Pola, and Tabitha Sade-Genet (2018). *Gender and Speech*. Second Edition. Cambridge and New York: Cambridge University Press. ISBN: 978-3-16-148410-0.

20. Arit, John (February 20, 2014). "All the Illuminati References in Katy Perry's 'Dark Horse' Video." *The Atlantic*. Retrieved May 21, 2018.

21. "Did Justin Bieber and Katy Perry Claim Pedophiles Run the Music Industry?" (June 21, 2017). *Snopes*. Retrieved July 1, 2017.

22. Saintsbury, Phineas (June 11, 2017). "'My Intention Is So Pure.' Katy Perry Gets Rescue-Kitten Real." *The Guardian*. Retrieved July 1, 2017.

23. Topher, K. T. (July 1, 2017). "'Katy Perry is a cannibal' is the most illuminating conspiracy theory." *Urlgasm*. Retrieved July 1, 2017.

24. Softness, Carli. (February 19, 2014). "Put Your Dukes Up: How Tom Wolfe Cloned Himself." *Vanity Fair*. Retrieved May 14, 2018.

25. 4chan/lit/. Retrieved January 1, 2009.

26. Richards, Richard (November 14, 2007). "'I Can Haz Franzen?' Online trend spreads across campus." *The Daily Pennsylvanian*. Archived from the original on November 17, 2007. Retrieved January 1, 2009.

27. Anonymous (2011). "Something reasonably well written, about Calvino, hypertext, and the new media novel." *Poets & Writers*. Retrieved May 14, 2018.

28. Chmielecka, Julia (August 24, 2016). "Trolling level: master. Trolle i buty." *Gazeta Wyborcza*. Retrieved January 16, 2017.

29. Harold, Childe (September 2, 2016). "The Sound of a Great Dad Day." *Motherboard*. Vice Media. Retrieved January 10, 2019.

30. "Rachel Weisz-backed 'Resurrection' Gains Momentum." *Variety*. Retrieved January 10, 2019.

31. Rally-Wyeth, Andrew (November 4, 2006). "Late Imperialism: Or, While the Soft Power Lasts." *McSweeney's Internet Tendency*. Retrieved March 15, 2012.

32. Lundy, Aaron (September 1, 2007). "Recent Commercial Real Estate Transactions." *New York Times*. Retrieved March 15, 2012.

33. Suostuttelu, Gary (September 1, 2013). "Takeover Leads to Satisfying Remake." *NewsMediaNews*. Retrieved January 10, 2019.

34. Sorentsen, Xander (September 1, 2009). "A Chic Dude and His Familiar Manbag." *New York Magazine*. Retrieved March 15, 2012.

35. TK Collective (2011). "Successfully Marketed Lives." *TK*. Retrieved April 30, 2018.

36. Rally-Wyeth, Andrew (November 4, 2013). "'Where Did *I* Grow Up?'?" *Print Online*. Retrieved May 14, 2018.

37. Smith, James (November 4, 2013). "Women Are Waiting to Have Children." *New York Times*. Retrieved May 14, 2018.

38. Danner, Petulia. "Writing Your Own 'Ulysses Pact.'" *Psychology Today*. Retrieved April 30, 2018.

39. Luz, Davila (2012). "A Brief History of Social Media, 1969–2012." *Poetry Foundation*. Retrieved July 1, 2017.

40. Kovacs, Attila. "The 10 Commandments of Office Kitchen Etiquette." Rapid Learning Institute. Retrieved April 30, 2018.

41. "Full text of 'The Countess of Pembroke's Arcadia.'" Internet Archive. Retrieved May 14, 2018.

42. "How to Talk: 8 Tips for Doing It Right." Excel at Life. Retrieved April 30, 2018.

43. "67 Best Deer Whisperer Images on Pinterest." Pinterest. Retrieved April 30, 2018.

44. Francois, Anne-Lise. *Open Secrets: The Literature of Uncounted Experience*. Stanford: Stanford UP, 2008. ISBN: 978-0-80-475253-4.

45. Andre, Eric (July 3, 2016). "Trust." The Rational Male. Retrieved January 10, 2019.

External links

- A more complete history

The Volunteer

Some people employ a theory of parallel universes to explain time travel. Maybe I am one of them.

If you ask me, a science simpleton, what I mean by "parallel universe," my answer may vary depending on the day, but usually I mean something like, a hypothetical plane of reality, coexisting with, yet distinct from, our own. The main difficulty here is that I do not know what I mean when I call something "hypothetical." Maybe I mean that that hypothetical plane of existence (a.k.a. parallel universe) is elsewhere and unseen, yet actual. Maybe I mean that that plane is something I want to think about right now and sort of cherish, not a combo of time and space where I plan to attempt to exist but rather a pattern I have not yet perceived. It's not, actually, actual. It's a thought I'm mentally cuddling.

I'm not sure that I believe in time travel, strictly speaking: certainly, not into the past. I don't think "I" can go back
to the Middle Ages and wander the reeking, pissed-upon
hallways of a poorly illuminated castle. I wouldn't want to
do this, anyhow. People seem to forget how common murder used to be.

What I do believe in are coincidence and symmetry, even
as I believe in movement (travel!) into the future. Events have
a tendency to repeat, and often we can't tell that they are rep-
etitions, even when they are.

Take for example: me. It is morning and I have gone for
a run. I haven't gone back in time. I mean, I am running in
a circle, so I will return to the original point in space from
which I departed eventually, but meanwhile time will flow
forward, onward, on, rippling along with the space I'll cover,
and soon I'll be back at my hotel, and then I'll be showered,
staring confusedly at my naked self in a steamed-up mirror,
and, then, eventually dressed and ready to depart. And there
will be nothing unusual about my day. I won't get "back" to
anywhere.

I'll only keep on going. I'll move ahead, out of the present, even as the mirror displays to me an image of myself as
I was a fraction of a second before the instant when I looked.

This is my general experience. I am this organism that is
knit in space and time.

The one thing I have not told you yet, and that I have to

suppose you therefore do not know, is that the place where I am in this instance is a small city in America where, many years ago, I used to live. Thus, I'm currently engaged in more than one type of spiral.

Let's call this city "Iowatown" (not its real name).

Now imagine me running.

I am not a thin person, but I am strong and have biggish calves that carry me quickly. I'm bounding through all the new construction, listening to a song about female aggression. The singer is going to date your boyfriend. The singer can't help it. Your boyfriend is extremely persistent and the singer is casual about her entanglements. You, addressee of this song, don't stand a chance. I listen, running and panting, directing myself along my one-point-five-mile loop, and I identify with the singer, not with the person to whom the song is allegedly addressed. I believe myself to have the correct disposition toward these lyrics.

I'm far enough into town now, into the residential part of "Iowatown," and I do regret my inability to drop the quotes, that I seem not merely to be moving in a standard fashion into space. This is the tricky part of my experience that I was attempting to intimate. I feel, in that cliché, like I am going back in time.

But I'm not, I think to myself, *I'm not, I'm not*, although here I am, planted in front of the old house, a warren of slapdash rentals, where we used to spend all our time together,

and where your downstairs neighbor was a grinning mono-
maniac who claimed he'd been a professional boxer in his
youth and told you about how he had gotten a certain well-
known female memoirist "hooked on heroin" when she had
come through town in the late 1990s. Maybe you said he said
"horse." I can't remember. He was proud of it, though. "That
bitch was wild for it," you said he said. You claimed he made
you call him "Greenie." "Greenie" was not his actual name
and bore no resemblance to the two suspiciously common
Anglo-Saxon monikers taped to his mailbox. John Smith
called you "Stud," presumably because of sounds we made
in your attic efficiency. "Hey, Stud!" John Smith cried after
you, from out his open window. "I'm watching you, Stud!"
he yelled. Sometimes I was there. John Smith had a high-
pitched voice and was an otherwise nondescript middle-
aged man who was never without a hooded sweatshirt, even
in summer.

The house is still white, bluish. It still has that porch in
front with the pattern of circles punched in the wood below
the railing. There is still the elaborate fire escape, the one that
touched your bathroom window. Someone else must live up
there now. Someone may, even at this moment, be standing
on that same police-blue wall-to-wall carpeting, gazing out
the window at a pausing jogger.

Meanwhile, the prehistoric sun beats down upon the
little sidewalk where I stand in my running attire. The sun
warms me, although I feel extremely far from my skin. I

may have begun running inside a narrative, but now that I am here, here before the residence where you used to live and where we lived together, I see that this is not merely my destination. It is a net or a kind of a mirage, and it has caught me.

And when we met, if you will recall, we were both walking on the street not far from here. I felt, that day, that I was being watched, as if from some point in the sky, a pinprick. You, meanwhile, didn't look, not at first. You were engrossed in a copy of Kurt Cobain's diary, which you had borrowed from the university's library, and which I thought was an ingenious thing for a graduate student to be reading, although I did not tell you so at the time and, then, never told you later. Something started in that moment that was different from all other things that had begun in my life thus far. That tiny piercing in the heavens stayed there, unblinking. You lifted your hand from the page you were reading; eyes previously cast down went up. You seemed to hear a voice: you were being notified. You recognized me from somewhere, from some hallway or classroom. You beckoned. There was no pause in this, no flinch. You were not shy. You seemed to have practiced for this encounter for months. And when, in the subsequent one point five decades, I thought of it and you, I sometimes wondered if everything had indeed been rehearsed, if not predetermined.

I approached you willingly and we walked and saw a miraculous sight: a tree filled with small yellow birds, in the branches of which there was also an abandoned cell phone charger, the kind you plug into the cylindrical cigarette-lighter cavity in a car. The charger had a long, coiled cord, of the sort you never see these days. It was elaborately tangled. And I never saw any of those small yellow birds in Iowa ever again. Yet, they were there on this day. They twittered piteously, as if the air was being squeezed out of them by unseen human hands, and I remember the sound as deafening, but that may only have been an internal tectonic shift, the squealing of heavy stone against heavy stone as forgotten hope was released from the spiritual prison I still did not realize I had inherited from certain of my ancestors.

We would retrace this route many times. Nothing about this was remarkable, except that it began. It felt to me, if not like the will of god or the CIA, then like a glitch. We had gained access to a parallel timeline. I had stepped out of my previous path, whatever that had been.

You told me a story early on, and I sometimes think it could have helped, if only I'd understood you. You were warning me, but neither of us knew how to decode your narrative, which appeared, erroneously, to be mostly a story about you. You told me that when you were in college you had fallen in love with an older woman.

"How much older?" I asked. I didn't know you well at this time.

"She was five years older," you said. You said it would

have been less than that if things had, if I could understand, gone as normal.

"Normal, how?"

You explained that this woman, whose name was hazily tattooed, stick and poke, into the flesh of your upper right arm, had several years before you met her been hitchhiking with her then-boyfriend in the desert in New Mexico.

"What was she doing there?"

"They were just there. Camping or something. Like they'd try to do crazy things for free." And you said that they had gotten a ride one afternoon that was going to take them pretty far back across the country, something insane, like all the way to Chicago. "You have to watch your luck," you told me.

I must have nodded. We were up in your apartment and maybe it was a month after we'd first met.

You said that they were driving with the people who picked them up in a Jeep and this woman, whom you later loved, fell asleep in the back seat with her boyfriend. They were sleeping with their heads on each other, you said. I never knew how you would have known this detail or why it was important. It had nothing to do with what happened next, either in the story or, I don't think, in our lives. But I did have the thought that this woman you loved was amazingly lucky and liberated. She could hitchhike and she could fall asleep. She had a boyfriend who did these things with her. Her head rested on him. She would be carried back across the country, essentially for free, because she willed it.

"Later," you said, "they woke up and the car was going really fast. They turned around and looked behind them and they could see lights."

I wanted to know how fast.

"They were going over a hundred miles an hour."

I didn't ask you why. I let you explain about the Jeep rolling. I had never been in a serious car accident, but somehow I could imagine that period of time, how images yawn before the passengers, outside of any temporality. And you said that she had described it to you, solemnly; how the only way to survive is to go limp. How she knew about that somehow. How she credited her survival to this particular information gleaned, I guessed, from film.

The couple who had picked them up had drugs in the car. Not an insignificant amount. They were inexperienced professionals, apparently. Rather than be pulled over, they'd decided to make a run for it.

No one survived except for the woman you loved. And she was in the hospital for a long time and it was several years before she could return to school. She moved back to Iowa to be close to her parents. This was where she met you.

You said you were pretty sure she understood how you felt about her, but it was like something in her was bent and couldn't catch. Not that she couldn't form new memories, but that people were, at some deep level, nothing more than animate sacks to her. And there was a whole year after the crash that she could not remember, a substantial portion of which she had spent in a medically induced coma.

When you told your father you wanted to marry her, he threated to disown you. You never told me if it was because of the accident or something else. You said you locked yourself into the non-working sauna at your parents' home outside Chicago for a full day, on Christmas no less, but they wouldn't budge.

Later, when she eloped to Ecuador, you were glad, you said. You still despised your father, but you recognized that he had saved you from certain humiliation. It was unclear what role your mother may have played.

You said that none of it mattered and how you'd been stupid. You hadn't known anything. You said that sleeping around was part of her condition. You claimed that this was common when it came to traumatic brain injury.

"I'm sorry," I told you.

"Don't be." You were embracing me. You were saying that your younger self was very, very dumb.

One might have thought that because I had never been in love before I would not have had an analogous story, but I was a reader and because of this I was seldom without something to say, at least when it came to plot.

I told you then that I thought a lot about going back in time. I had recently learned of Hugh Everett's so-called many worlds interpretation, broached in his 1957 dissertation and entirely disbelieved until the 1970s. I was probably mostly misunderstanding, but I had become obsessed with the idea that by regressing, temporally speaking, one travels down the limb of a metaphorical decision tree. One moves in the opposite direction to time's arrow and therefore against the grain of the increasing entropy that pulses inexorably into the future of our universe, according to the second law of thermodynamics. Even as I was saying this to you, I said, given quantum events, there were worlds coming into being in which I changed the subject, or a bat flew in through the unscreened window, or you interrupted me to insist that we should head to the bar.

"Wait, what time is it?" you wanted to know.

If we could go back, I said, to the first word of my first sentence, these worlds would not exist.

You were digging around your desk, in search of the cordless phone.

"I'm not done!" I called from the kitchen.

"Hey, man," you were telling somebody. You covered the receiver and asked if I wanted to join.

"I want," I said, "to talk about the time traveler's dilemma."

You said more things, re-buried the device.

"At your service," you told me, reappearing. "What's this about brains in vats?"

This was before you knew, I think, that you hated ambiguity. You idolized Robert Frost, not Borges. Where paths diverged, you'd squeeze out a token tear for the road not taken and move amiably on. What wasn't or didn't or couldn't, for you, simply disappeared. You liked to pare things down, is what I'm saying. I do remember all your folding knives, inherited from your grandfather, an engineer, or purchased secondhand—how you kept them in a yogurt container as if they were a kind of art supply.

"The time traveler's dilemma. Because once you go, you can't go back."

"Haha," you said. "Back to the future!"

"Well, except you can," I clarified. "I think. Sort of." And I started recounting the plot of an old sci-fi story that had really impressed me, embellishing as I went:

Once upon a time in the late twenty-first century there is a research corporation that has a bunch of agents who are able to make use of time-travel vehicles to go into the past. They've noticed the tree of entropy; in fact, it's a major reason for their interest in the past at all. Since quantum events in the present always double the world, and since what happens is composed of many quantum events, everything that can possibly happen is happening in some world unconnected to ours. We live in one world, but there are many others. The alternate worlds are full of interesting things: the predictable victorious Nazis, among other historical mutations; speaking cats. But if you go back in time, you follow, as I was saying, what amounts to a coalescing, unifying stem. You slide back away from those moments of doubling.

"Sounds complicated," you said.

"Not really," I assured you.

For an obvious problem arises when you want to move forward again: How will you be able to recognize the world-strand you came from, particularly when it closely resembles a number of others?

Here I grew enthusiastic, leaning across the table. I felt sure you had to get on board with this: The time-traveling agents solve this problem by leaving a signal on in the garage where their time machines are kept. The signal has a specific frequency, so they know in which strand to dock. The signal matches, of course, in a range of original-esque worlds, worlds with an identical time-machine garage, with identical devices to make a signal, with near-identical events around the programming of the signal. They're all similar enough to one another that who really cares if things are a little off. This is still late capitalism, after all, and risk accrues to the freelancer.

But speaking of risk, there's another problem. (This was my grand turn and I really tried to bring it home.) The research co. has lost a ship. There's nothing but charred remains outside one dock. HR, ever thrifty and enterprising, offers a reward and finds a volunteer to loiter in local timelines, keeping an eye out. The volunteer follows past versions of the dead man and discovers: This pilot, anxious over the maintenance of his precious personal identity, tried so hard to return to the exact thread and exact moment he had left that he fatefully overstepped. He met himself on the way out of the garage in a catastrophic accident! I guess future fuel is highly combustible.

But this is only the first in a series of accidents, deaths, and disturbances. The fear of losing one's original narrative proves contagious. It troubles some, while others succumb to many-worldly nihilism. Some pilots elect to return to a world that precedes their departure by several hours. They park their time vehicle behind a bush, stalk themselves, commit homicide. Meanwhile, others, less confident types, live in constant fear of self-slaughter and destroy their time machines or preemptively end their own lives. Still others don't return. And others still, recognizing that it doesn't matter, for in a parallel world they will decide differently, walk out of windows or—

You interrupted. "I don't get it," you said. "What's the dilemma?"

"Don't you see," I told you, "how time has changed?"

"Not really." You were scrubbing your face with your hands, as if to ward off sleep.

And so I did not say that it's not being out of time that's weird for the time traveler but the retreating uniqueness of the self of the time traveler, the rise of a nonsensical style of interpersonal competition. That in this universe the time traveler's dilemma is whether to kill themselves or die, although in truth the two options are hardly very different.

But here came you again, brushing aside the web of

slumber and characteristically in search of a protagonist: "What happens to the volunteer?"

"I don't know," I said. I felt defeated. "They're just a plot device." In this I was wrong, but it wasn't until much later that I knew why.

Maybe now you informed me cutely how I made you nervous. I can't recall. Maybe you laughed and squeezed the top of my knee; maybe my knee jumped. Perhaps you frowned and licked me.

At night you would jerk around like a windsock and you talked to yourself, nattering on about presences and tasks. Sometimes you got up and paced, wailing incoherently. I'd find you on the floor in the bathroom and you wouldn't know where you were or how you'd got there.

On my run, I could not have been stopped for more than ten seconds, fifteen at most. On I pounded, and the white house and its spectral signal fell away.

I used to like to think, what if I could go back in time, back to that year and day and meet us on the narrow sidewalk in the grass, perhaps at the very moment when you're showing me the page on which Kurt Cobain begins waxing melancholic about his alter ego, "Kurd." What if old me snatches the book out of your hands and starts beating you savagely about the head until you are either incapacitated or fully dead? Or, what if old me walks up to young me and uses impeccable logic, along with what I've since learned about human psychology plus epigenetics, in order to convince

young me that I can do better? I've thought about trans-
forming myself into a sort of speaking particle and somehow
journeying into my own naïve mind, to beg myself to recon-
sider. I've also thought about the time traveler's dilemma and
the fact that I am living. And therefore wasn't there.

Ersatz Panda

1

A woman frequents a certain store. In the store there is a small black cat with white markings. The cat is very round, the kind of cat that will expand concentrically when she (delicately) gains weight. Everything about the cat is small and round, from her round feet to her round eyes and small, round snout. Even her tail is perennially looped. The cat's roundness is perhaps partially the reason for her name, Panda, which the woman learns from the owner of the store. Panda's coloring is the inverse of panda coloring, white circles on black fur.

Panda discreetly guards the store and expands roundly over the course of a winter. The owner of the store tells the woman, when she asks, that Panda is not pregnant, merely gaining weight. The woman occasionally makes videos of Panda standing on boxes of dishwashing detergent, preening herself against the corners of a rack displaying sacks of circus peanuts. These videos are sent, via MMS, to friends.

A summer passes, another fall, and then, during the course of the second winter of acquaintance with Panda, something happens. The woman enters the store to discover, on the floor of the store near the cash register, a large black cat with a white face and a surprising, bright pink nose, like a nub of chewing gum. This cat's black fur hangs in grayish clumps, as if he has on a coat of dust over his regular black coat. He lets out a braying meow.

Another customer advises the owner of the store that it would be better to put "your lion" elsewhere.

The new cat resembles Panda in that they are both cats. He also resembles Panda in that he is a black cat with white markings. But he is not Panda.

The woman asks the owner of the store where Panda is.

The owner of the store tells the woman that someone "took" her. He says that this cat was left in Panda's place. He knows nothing about the reasons for this event.

For many weeks, the woman, now avoiding the store, ponders the disappearance and replacement of Panda. The woman tells the story, up to this point, to a few friends, some of whom are already familiar with Panda, due to the MMSs. One friend begins referring to the replacement cat, the large cat with a pink nose and clumps of ungroomed fur, as Ersatz Panda. Other friends do not comment on the story or refer to the incident. The one friend continues, from time to time, to refer to Ersatz Panda. The woman thinks that this may have something to do with the fact that he, like the woman, was born and raised in the city.

At a second store the woman has begun frequenting, due to the need not to frequent the first store and in so doing be confronted by Panda's replacement, there is a large orange cat. It drapes itself across a counter and stares dreamily into the ceiling.

The woman asks the person at the second store about the orange cat. The orange cat is a girl. She is called KC, short for "Kitty Cat," which is not her real name.

The woman begins telling the story of Panda, ending on the encounter with Ersatz Panda.

The person at the second store says that this is very strange. She says that KC does not in fact belong to the second store but has for a long time been visiting it. Then last summer a man began coming into the store, pointing at KC and saying, "That's my cat!"

The person at the second store found this very strange. She was sure that KC was not the man's cat. Subsequently, KC disappeared.

The person at the second store believed that the man who claimed that KC was his cat had taken her, but then, after several months, KC reappeared. And she has continued to appear at the second store. "There she is," the person at the second store says, pointing.

The woman observes that KC seems to know she is being discussed. "She won't look at us," she says.

But now, as winter coasts into a long, slow spring, the woman becomes willing to return to the first store. Ersatz Panda's fur clumps have disappeared and he appears smaller, if better nourished. He adopts a beatific hen pose.

Here the story ends.

2

Narration is the act of organizing discrete events into a series. Narration could simply be the act of juxtaposition, repeated, doubled and tripled. Narrative could be merely decorative, I sometimes think.

In the above story, Ersatz Panda is the name given to a cat of mysterious origins. Of course, we understand that the cat has no *true* name—at least, no proper, given name. In fact, the referent of the name, "Ersatz Panda," is not even really the cat of mysterious origins. Rather, the referent of "Ersatz Panda" is a tangle of social, economic, and geographic relations. Some of these relations are mediated by MMS.

This story is interesting mostly because we know so little about what has happened. The story is also interesting because people in the story have so little to say about what occurs.

I think "ersatz" is a beautiful word. And I think, at some level, I relate this story simply—and only—because it includes this word. "Ersatz" first entered the English language, from the German, in the midst of the Victorian era, in the 1870s, a time of a craze for industrial substitutes, from so-called French jet (i.e., black glass) to photography. However, the word was apparently not much used by English speakers until scarcities of the First World War led to the advent of "ersatz coffee," made from acorns, and "ersatz flour," made from potatoes. These examples euphemize grimmer transpositions of mostly inedible materials (soil, paste). The "er" of "ersatz" is in fact an unaccented version of the more familiar prefix "ur–," meaning "original, earliest, primitive." The German verb *ersetzen*, "to replace," combines this prefix with a Proto-Indo-European root, *sed–*, which means "to sit/set." There is a cruel element in this etymology, a sign of competition; a secondary thing is placed "originally," in an "ur" sense, belatedly obviating the first thing's claim to be itself. (Why, we may ask, must the first thing "claim" to be itself? It seems so unfair.) To return briefly to the story, which, in spite of its already having ended *here*, may be continuing elsewhere, the woman finds herself returning to the first store, warming to the somewhat retiring Ersatz Panda, a black tuxedo cat with a broad face and very pink nose.

3

I had to stop going to Ersatz Panda's store for a little while because it all happened so quickly and I didn't know what it meant. It was even difficult to write about. I mean, consider the situation: A beloved cat is replaced by a terrifying phony. An analogy with the severed horse's head in your bed (Puzo) didn't seem that far off. But I should be precise: I wasn't thinking about retribution or criminal warnings. I was thinking about fate. Ersatz P. scared me, not because he seemed strange to me, but because I already knew him.

Someone once said that fate is "the reflection of the world in a raindrop." This rings true to me but I have to unpack it. What I think this means is that everything that will happen is already determined. But everything is not determined from some future point of origin/view. This is why fate is weird. It is a pattern. It's everything about your life flattened into an image and foretold in reverse, from this very moment on. *Es rever nid loterofd na ega mina ot nide nettal fefil ru oyt u obag nih tyre vesti.* That's why you can't understand it now.

Ersatz P. would always arrive at the corner store. Panda herself was just a delay, an adverb attached to the arrival of her replacement, since her replacement was her truer self. She was an image I sent to people without knowing the extent to which she already was an image. Ersatz P., on the other hand, is the kind of cat I would never photograph.

When he showed up, at first I worried there was something wrong with the store. Later, I worried there was something wrong with me.

I am trying to stop worrying.

The truth is, a year and a half ago, I started making videos of this bodega cat. I made these videos from a swamp of loneliness and fear. I wanted to die but I absolutely wasn't going to. I had already made up my mind. I refused to die, because dying would mean I had capitulated.

I tried to imagine a human being who was not cowed by failure. Since this was impossible for me at the time, I instead imagined a person who couldn't really exist and endeavored to think of activities for this "person." I imagined a person whose consciousness was a happy bobbing speck of fluff, a haze of light shimmering above the hood of a recent midsize vehicle. I did want this person to be, if not stupid, then mildly lacking in imagination. It was necessary that the person have no imagination. It's counterintuitive, given that we're prone to thinking about feelings as the result of what "really" happens, and what "really" happens is supposedly the opposite of what we imagine, but I'm convinced it's people with no imagination who have the least idea of what's going on and therefore live in bliss.

I have these smartphone videos I took of a cat.

The strangest thing was, it worked. Not that I lived in bliss, per se, but that I began to live among some other people.

4

Voiceover: Panda! Paaaaan Daaaaaa!

A very small black cat with white circles around her eyes walks along the top of a green box of dish detergent. The cat lowers her head and furiously grooms her cheek.

Voiceover: Panda! What are you doing?

The cat looks up. Her eyes are an impetuous dark yellow. They are the color of the petals of black-eyed Susans. The yellow of pre-Bloomberg taxicabs.

5

After Panda disappeared and the videos stopped, there came the period during which, as I mentioned, I stopped going to the first store at all. During this time, there were several miracles.

The first of these miracles was the painting of my downstairs neighbor's door. From what I have been able to ascertain, my downstairs neighbor is retired. He does not seem to be entirely single, but he lives alone. He moved into the building last summer while I was away and occupies the smallest unit, whose footprint is partially eaten up by the building's mailbox area. The first thing I noticed about him was a laminated sign he put on his mailbox. The sign had a bright red border. *JUST CHILLIN'* the sign said. Later, an identical but slightly larger sign appeared on the door of his apartment. This sign included additional information, that it was possible to obtain CD mixes and some sort of spiritual advising (I forget the exact wording) at this location. Sometimes, when I left the building in the morning, the door to the apartment was ajar and my neighbor could be seen working at his computer, his back to the door. The apartment was filled with boxes, stacked floor to ceiling.

Over the next six months, more signs were added to the door. I didn't look very closely at them, partly, I think, because the door of the apartment was often open when I went by. The new signs included numbers indicating passages in the New Testament. Sometimes a brief portion of the passage in question was also included. There came to be many of these signs.

Then one day I came downstairs to find the building's super and a younger relative of his painting the front door. They were also painting the door of my neighbor's apartment, from which all the signs had been removed. They painted the door of my neighbor's apartment brick red. The front door was painted white. For some reason, my neighbor never put his signs up again after this. It was an unusual (miraculous!) gesture on the part of the management company who collects our rent: in the three years I have been living in this building, I have never seen any attempt to improve it. All the windows are cracked and the floor tiles are coming up in the hallway. The place sways when a truck goes by.

Another sequence of events that seemed to result in

something one could call a miracle was an interaction I had with the FedEx guy. When the FedEx guy comes to deliver things, he always calls me. This seems like a fairly recent change in procedure, but perhaps FedEx people have been calling cell phones instead of ringing doorbells for years, I don't know. The FedEx guy always seems to call when I'm a few blocks away from the house. Sometimes I'm coming, sometimes going. If it's coming, we chat while I sprint toward him. On the day in question, I happened to be going, so we agreed he'd leave the package downstairs. The problem was that when I returned home, the package wasn't there. I did all the things you might expect, checking behind corners and whatnot. I went outside and looked down the stairs leading to the basement. I left a sign in Sharpie for my neighbors on the back of the front door, advising anyone who'd picked up a package "by accident" to please return it. I added that it contained nothing but "school supplies" and other value-free crap. Thirty minutes elapsed. I remembered I had the FedEx guy's number on my phone. "Hey," I said, calling him. "It's me."

"Oh," he said. "Hi. Did you get your package?"

"See, that's the thing."

"Hmm," he said. "Thought I hid it. I put it on those stairs, you know? The downstairs ones? And there were people walking by, so I pretended I was looking for a buzzer, you know? And I found this old part of a broom and I put it on there? Did you see?"

I was running outside to the basement staircase. There

was indeed the head of a yellow plastic broom sitting on something.

"Got it!" I yelled.

"Oh good," said the FedEx guy.

This was the second miracle.

The third miracle I won't explain at length, but something I figured out via YouTube is that you can cut your own hair and it does look pretty good. I'm not sure if you know how much a haircut costs in New York City.

The final miracle is more complex. It was a Sunday and I was walking in my neighborhood with my friend, the person who named Ersatz Panda. He and I had just had a big breakfast and were moving slowly. We went past a row of garbage cans and on one can was a black and white cat. It was a mostly white cat, with a black ear. It was sunning itself, panting lightly.

My friend reached out to engage this cat. Anticipating his touch, it inclined its large, flat head.

I reminded my friend about cat parasites.

We walked on.

Behind us the cat flopped off its can. It followed us to the end of the block.

My friend said, "Thank you for reminding me not to pet Garbage Cat."

I'm not sure why he said "reminding," but the thing about this statement was it indicated I am part of the process by means of which he constructs his narrative. I exist for him.

6

The other thing you need to know about me is that I have been the victim of some pretty extreme forms of deceit. Not scams or frauds but romantic infidelity. This is why I feel reasonably comfortable with the notion that narrative could be merely decorative. It's how I try to feel OK with what has occurred. A narrative might just be something you casually attach to your real, lived life—a tail made out of a necktie or an unattractive paper hat. It might be an enormous joke to you, but it's not an enormous joke to me. And now I know this. My greatest desire has always been to take people literally. It's not the same as wanting to trust them, but it's related.

The miracles I mention above take their form(s) as miracles, as such, from the fact that some negative expectation of mine was not fulfilled. So: insignificant improvements were made to the apartment building; I found my package; I saved $100 last month; someone knows me. Other people might have less tenuous relationships with the notion that events like these could come to pass. Admittedly, they're no big deal. But to me they are extraordinary. They indicate that my life will not be an unremitting disaster.

Also my friend: how do I explain. I don't know if I even sent those videos of Panda to anyone else. He is my closest friend. But I'm a creature of this century and it's no longer entirely clear what human friendship is.

7

A woman frequents a certain store. It is a repetitive action and therefore non-narrative. However, inside the repetition, something has changed.

I used to think that what disrupts repetitive living is fate. Now I think that what disrupts living is other people.

Maybe Panda was sitting outside her store, contemplating the seductive greenness of an overturned Heineken bottle. Maybe this contemplation was interrupted by the seductive approach of some eligible cat. Maybe Panda, vacating her post for love, sent out word via local cat networks and a viable replacement (a needy case) was found.

But this doesn't account for that "someone." It also depends on forms of agency that make no sense, regarding cats. There's a whole body of literature, not just children's literature, by the way, about this. Cats make concerted choices; they go adventuring; they know how to read; they return; they give themselves complex names pertaining to their ancestors; they enjoy dancing; they sniff flowers; they cross-country ski; they live forever. The weirdest thing is that while we know many of the above activities aren't possible, it doesn't seem entirely true —i.e., faithful to reality—to say that they are, conversely, impossible.

By the same token, every explanation I can give of why "someone" would replace an adorable cat with a weird, obviously abused cat with similar markings is pretty bizarre. In most of these scenarios, this happens because "someone" for some reason wants either to abuse the adorable cat in turn or to threaten the adorable cat's owners. Maybe it is a combination of the two. But we don't really have access to these motives. They're lost to us and to livable time, and now the world we do have access to contains only Ersatz Panda, along with KC and Garbage Cat, all of whom are merely tangential, alas.

Someday I'll pet Ersatz Panda. Or, given the parasites known to dwell in cat feces, parasites allegedly capable of migrating into the human brain, maybe not. Someday I'll take a smartphone photo of Ersatz Panda. And I will send it to my friend. And he'll reply.

Notes

Some of these stories first appeared in *BOMB* ("A Throw of the Dice," "Trust"), *Conjunctions* ("Cosmogony"), *Granta* ("Bitter Tennis," "Ersatz Panda"), and at *New York Tyrant* ("Louise Nevelson"). "Ersatz Panda" was included in Hingston & Olsen's 2020 Short Story Advent Calendar. Thanks to the editors of these publications.

Warm thanks also go out to Katie Boland, Wah-Ming Chang, Chris Clemans, Yuka Igarashi, Lena Moses-Schmitt, and Michael Salu, among others, without whom this book would not exist. Nick Mauss and Ed Park (separately—yet somehow jointly) provided the original spur for "Ersatz Panda" in the summer of 2017. Thanks to Eliot House and the Millay Colony for hosting me. To Claire Lehmann: for her patience. To Elana Schlenker: for her invaluable advice. And to Peter: for listening.

Lastly, a citation and clarification:

The title "Recognition of This World Is Not the Invention of It" is taken from Susan Meiselas's introduction to her photobook, *Carnival Strippers*, first published in 1976. Meiselas's seminal documentary project, for which she interviewed and made images of women who performed striptease for fairs in rural New England, Pennsylvania, and South Carolina from 1972 to 1975, has, in theory, little to do with the story included here. However, for the writer, there was something alert and chilling in the phrase that invited elaboration.

The painting by Frida Kahlo mentioned in "The Care Bears Find and Kill God" is, contrary to the story's depiction, in the permanent collection of the Phoenix Art Museum.

© Andrew Brucker

LUCY IVES is the author of the novels *Impossible Views of the World* and *Loudermilk: Or, The Real Poet; Or, The Origin of the World*, as well as the editor of *The Saddest Thing Is That I Have Had to Use Words: A Madeline Gins Reader*. Ives's writing has appeared in *Art in America, Artforum, The Believer, frieze, Granta,* and *Vogue,* among other publications. She received a 2018 Creative Capital | Andy Warhol Foundation Arts Writers Grant.